BEOWULF
ORACLE

WISDOM FROM
THE NORTHERN KINGDOMS

BEOWULF
ORACLE

WISDOM FROM
THE NORTHERN KINGDOMS

JOHN MATTHEWS | VIRGINIA CHANDLER
illustrated by
JOE MACHINE

"Kennings" by
CAITLÍN MATTHEWS

Foreword by
DIANA L. PAXSON

REDFeather™
MIND | BODY | SPIRIT

4880 Lower Valley Road, Atglen, PA 19310

Other REDFeather Books
by the Author:
The Grail Tarot: A Templar Vision,
John Matthews, with cards illustrated by
Giovanni Caselli, ISBN 978-0-7643-5892-0

*The Byzantine Tarot: Wisdom from an Ancient
Empire*, John Matthews & Cilla Conway,
ISBN 978-0-7643-6041-1

Other REDFeather Books
on Related Subjects:
The Promethean Oracle,
Sophia Kelly Shultz and Mark Cogan,
ISBN 978-0-7643-5407-6

The Ring Cycle Tarot, Allegra Printz, cards
adapted from the illustrations of Arthur
Rackham, ISBN 978-0-7643-4817-4

The Gorgon's Tarot, Dolores Fitchie,
ISBN 978-0-7643-4590-6

Library of Congress Control Number:
2021931777

"Red Feather Mind Body Spirit" logo is a
trademark of Schiffer Publishing, Ltd.
"Red Feather Mind Body Spirit Feather"
logo is a registered trademark of Schiffer
Publishing, Ltd.

Cover and interior design by
Brenda McCallum
Type set in Romance Fatal/Optima
ISBN: 978-0-7643-6250-7
Printed in China

Published by Red Feather Mind, Body, Spirit
An imprint of Schiffer Publishing, Ltd.
4880 Lower Valley Road
Atglen, PA 19310
Phone: (610) 593-1777;
Fax: (610) 593-2002
E-mail: Info@schifferbooks.com
Web: www.redfeathermbs.com

For our complete selection of fine books
on this and related subjects, please visit our
website at www.schifferbooks.com. You may
also write for a free catalog.

REDFeather's titles are available at special
discounts for bulk purchases for sales
promotions or premiums. Special editions,
including personalized covers, corporate
imprints, and excerpts, can be created in
large quantities for special needs. For more
information, contact the publisher.

We are always looking for people to write
books on new and related subjects. If you
have an idea for a book, please contact us at
proposals@schifferbooks.com.

"Always, a hero comes home."
Lyric from "A Hero Comes Home," by Alan Silvestri,
Soundtrack to *Beowulf* (2007)

To Neil Gaiman, whose solution to parts of the story in his script for the 2007 movie of *Beowulf* inspired me to create this oracle, and to Caitlín, for always being a steady hand on the tiller of my life.

—John Matthews

To that unnamed skald who first composed *Beowulf* so many years ago, your words have inspired me since my first reading. To Melody for her unwavering support and love.

—Virginia Chandler

I would like to thank John Matthews and his tremendous work as the source of inspiration for the illustrations. I dedicate this series to my dear son Finn, a true hero of the old tradition.

—Joe Machine

ACKNOWLEDGMENTS

Our first and biggest thank-you goes to Joe Machine, who took on this task with ease and courtesy and produced some of the most amazing imagery we could have imagined. A big thank-you also to Caitlín Matthews, who helped us out at a moment when the whole oracle seemed to be falling apart, and for the remarkable kennings, which appeared as if by magic and were so perfect we kept them in. To David E. for reading some of the chapters and spotting a few howlers. Any remaining errors are ours, of course. Thanks also to Saivite W., whose knowledge of runes made our task so much easier. And of course, to everyone at REDFeather for their work on the package and for making our work lighter by their expertise.

John Matthews, Oxford, England
Virginia Chandler, Atlanta, Georgia, USA
Joe Machine, Somerset, England

CONTENTS

FOREWORD

Hwaet! So! Listen up!

Thus does the poet of *Beowulf* compel our attention as he begins his tale. Like the chroniclers of the Norse sagas, although with rather more ornament, he launches his account with the backstory of Scyld Scefing and his heirs, culminating in the building of a "mightier house for mead-drinking than the children of men had ever known." In this Migrations Period epic, Hrothgar's construction of Heorot is an act of hubris whose equal and opposite reaction is the emergence of Grendel from the mists of a more primal world. The story of *Beowulf* comes to us from the peoples who gave us the English language. A vocabulary of archetypes connects us to a deeper level of the soul. The language of legend still speaks to us today.

As we seek oracles to guide our own evolution, we become the hero, but as the summary in chapter 2 of this book explains, the epic has two parts. *Beowulf* is first the story of an individual, a hero who challenges fate alone. His task is to help a kinsman by defeating Grendel, but his goal is to win honor, to achieve self-realization in the context of his personal goals. The second part of the story has a different focus. The story of Beowulf's conflict with the dragon shows him as a king whose first responsibility is to his kingdom. Individual achievement is not enough. The deeds of the mature hero are meaningful because they serve the community.

The oracle cards will introduce you not only to Beowulf himself, but to other legendary characters with whom he interacts both in pursuit of his own evolution and his service to his community. Interacting with the cards, you will enter that world and not only learn more about yourself but absorb the values and worldview of the peoples of the North Sea coasts whose culture was one of the primary ancestors of our own.

As you work with the *Beowulf Oracle*, I encourage you to further explore its sources. There are many translations of the original poem, from Seamus Meaney's Anglo-Irish version to the slangy recent interpretation by Maria Dahvana Headley. Of those listed at the end of this book, my favorite is the one by J. R. R. Tolkien, who as holder of the Chair for Anglo-Saxon at Oxford had an exhaustive understanding of the language, and as author of *The Lord of the Rings* (and a good poet himself) had explored what it means to be a hero, or a king. My favorite fictional version of the poem is *Beowulf* by Stephan Grundy (available from Amazon on Kindle), a gripping retelling that gives the best (that I have found) historical picture of the culture in which the original events would have taken place.

May the hero's path lead you to victory!

—Diana L. Paxson, author of *Taking Up the Runes*, *The Way of the Oracle*, and the Wodan's Children trilogy.

INTRODUCTION

A BRIEF HISTORY OF THE POEM

The epic poem *Beowulf* is known to the modern world thanks to a thousand-year-old manuscript that can still be seen at the British Museum in London. Although damaged by fire in 1731, the manuscript is still in good condition. Why or how the poem was selected to be written down is unknown. Indeed, how the recorders were familiar with this tale in the first place is still a mystery. Who were they? Why *Beowulf*?

Taking into account the age of the actual parchment, the manuscript itself dates to the late tenth or early eleventh century. On the basis of what we know of that period of British history, most scholars believe that one, or perhaps more, Anglo-Saxon Christian monks were the recorders of *Beowulf*. It is also generally understood that these scribes interjected some rather jarring and very specific Christian lines into the epic tale as they wrote down the words. The "why" of that is fairly obvious: they were obligated to connect any successful hero to the power of their god. Furthermore, any villains would also need to be tethered to the Christian mythos.

Yet, the story is set in northern Europe and tells the story of a mighty warrior hero who exhibits the ethos of a pre-Christian, Scandinavian culture. There is nothing Christian about Beowulf or his companions, not in what they say or in what they do. The monsters that they face come from a world where trolls haunt the moors and dragons are truly feared. There are kings, queens, and heroes in *Beowulf* that appear in other Scandinavian texts as well: Hrothgar, Hrothulf, Halfdane, and Froda can all be found in the Norse-Icelandic *Eddas*. It would make sense, then, that the story of Beowulf, the warrior hero, is much, much older than the tenth or eleventh century. In fact, it may be from as long ago as the fourth or fifth century.

Bo Gräslund, a retired archeology professor at Uppsala University in Sweden, proposed in spring 2019 that the poem is Scandinavian in origin and probably six hundred years older than is currently accepted.[1] The pre-Christian culture so clearly described in the poem includes many Scandinavian tribes: Danes, Jutes, Geats, and Waegmundings, to name a few. Professor Gräslund suggests that *Beowulf* offers valuable knowledge about Scandinavia's early history and was composed hundreds of years before the Christian monks wrote it all down.

If the tale of Beowulf and the monsters is indeed as old as the fourth century, then that would put it firmly in the heart of pre-Christian Scandinavia. It would also strongly suggest that the Christian elements are a much-later addition to the story and do not belong at all.

Reclaiming *Beowulf* as a Scandinavian epic and returning the story to its roots allows a certain very old, very ancient flavor to seep back into the tale. It is this ancient energy that inspired the skalds of old to first compose the story of Beowulf; it is this ancient energy that also inspired what you have before you, *The Beowulf Oracle*. For those who are less familiar with the poem, we have included a prose retelling. We suggest you read this at least once before you begin working with the oracle.

---

1   In an interview with the SVT, Professor Gräslund explained that Beowulf was composed before Nordic people used written language. It was later written down in full in an English monastery. How the poem reached England is unknown, but Professor Gräslund thinks this could have happened during a wedding between an East Anglian king and a princess from present-day Sweden.

FATE, SKALDS, AND GLORIOUS DEATH

"Cattle die, kinsmen die; the self must also die. I know one thing which never dies: the reputation of each dead man," from *The Havamal*, translated by Jackson Crawford (Crawford, 2015)

The world of the epic poem *Beowulf* is rich with beautiful, alliterative language that evokes vivid imagery of dragons, hags, and heroes. *The Beowulf Oracle* was born from this magical world and adventurous spirit. The Scandinavian tribes' belief in the journey each of us takes to achieve immortality is at the heart of this oracle. Along with the strong belief in Fate, the oracle also emphasizes the power of the Viking skald.

The skald used very specific techniques in their craft, including the arrangement of the words of the song or poem. This verse form is called *fornyrðislag*, which translates to "the ancient way of words." This "way of ancient words" was and is much more than simply a form of alliteration and verse; this weaving of words is a tool that was (and can still be) used by the skalds to transform language into energy. We believe that the words of *Beowulf* (sans the added Christian elements) are also empowered with *fornyrðislag*.

To appreciate the full power of the "way of ancient words" is to *feel* it. Unlike bards and scops, the Scandinavian skalds were seldom accompanied by a stringed musical instrument—nor did they sing as we would understand that type of performance. A drum or rattle might accompany the skald's words, but it was the skald's voice that held the power and wove the words into this flavor of magic.

The purpose of skaldic poetry also differed from the simpler, Eddic verse, which usually told the tales of the gods. The skalds' verse was focused on the heroic deeds of a warrior or jarl. This homage was most likely considered to be a vital element of the path to Scandinavian immortality via *Glorious Death*.

Skaldic poetry primarily employed *dróttkvætt*, an eight-line stanza with every two lines connected, but rather than depending on the poetic meter or a rhyming pattern, the skalds used alliteration to emphasize syllables and sounds to invoke a particular sensory experience for their audience. Along with this incredible emphasis on sound, a skald would add another magical element to the poetic charm: the *kenning*.

The kenning was used to invoke a particular image for those who heard the skald's performance. These metaphors required both clever wordplay and word skill. The kenning could be considered as a two-word riddle (or linked collection of riddles) designed to create a specific mental image that is held in common by a clan or people. Rather than use the word for "ocean" or "sea," a skald wove the image of a hero's voyage across the ocean with "whale-road" or "sail's way." A ship would become a "sea-steed," and the sun became a "sky-candle." By emphasizing certain syllables, using alliteration to harness the power of sound, and invoking magical images in the form of kennings, the skald became a weaver of worlds where their voice literally created magic.

As you read the words that we have been inspired to include as part of this oracle, it is the clear, strong voice of a skald that we hope you will hear. If that is not your experience at first, then it is our intention that *The Beowulf Oracle* will lead you to that inner, spiritual place.

We are not suggesting that the Viking skald who first composed this hero's tale was a rune magician, seer, or *völva*; nor are we suggesting that *Beowulf* was composed or performed as a magical ritual. What we are presenting through *The Beowulf Oracle* is a familiar heroic adventure that we believe can be used by the seeker as a tool to gain insight and guidance for their own life's journey. As the song composed by Alan Silvestri for the soundtrack of the 2007 film *Beowulf*, which we placed at the front of this book, says: *"Always a hero comes home."* This may sometimes be in spirit only, but in the context of the journeys undertaken here, you—as heroes—will always return.

What should we say about the Scandinavian belief in Fate? How does it factor into this oracle? It certainly cannot be ignored, since Fate was indeed a powerful, unmoving force in the world of *Beowulf*. Yet, even though the skein of life had been woven, it is written in the sagas and *Eddas* that mortals still sought the seers, or *völvas*, to seek hints of what was to come. The foolish mortal who tried to outwit or change Fate was certainly doomed. Even the gods who attempted to change what Fate had decreed failed. In the vast world of the Norse Viking, Fate is indeed set, but it can also be *seen*.

How does seeing what Fate has woven aid the seeker if he or she cannot change it? First, it is rare that the entirety of a seeker's life will be revealed through vision or divination. So, it would be unwise to assume that what is revealed by *The Beowulf Oracle*, or by any oracle, is the fully woven tapestry of one's life. Second, it is a gift from the gods that some portion of the seeker's Fate may be revealed; the seeker would be wise to take this knowledge and use it as a tool to prepare for what is ahead. Finally, since our oracle presents a hero's journey, it reveals *where* the seeker is on the path, and *what* or *who* is influencing the journey. It is a "Seeing" that the gods have chosen to reveal; it is a "Knowing" of what is to come.

Truly, if the seeker has any misgivings concerning what might be revealed, then the seeker should, quite frankly, abandon their efforts to "see" and "know." Nor is it needful that the seeker believe, implicitly, in the gods named here. The revealing of Fate should not be taken lightly. As *Beowulf* tells us, "Fate will often save an uncursed man, if his strength is constant."

Courage then, seeker, in your quest!

THE STORY OF BEOWULF RETOLD

The night was as dark and drenching as deep winter's whale road. The only promise of warmth and refuge from the bone-chilling night was the high hall of Hrothgar, the hearth of Heorot.

Grendel dared not seek shelter within those walls, though. The blood feud that began with his act of kin-slaying had caused son and mother to be exiled from all clans. Nameless they were now; called only grinder and grinder's kin. Their rage was fed by Grendel's bloody deeds. Revenge ever his only thought, Grendel relished his savage war with the Danes.

If he could not be made welcome and enjoy the hearth and courtesy of Hrothgar's great hall, it was only a minor mindset to thoughts of murder. There would be no man price for what he would do to mighty Heorot. Hrothgar's warriors would die while the old king lingered, stalked and then slaughtered within the walls of the Danes' beloved home.

For many grim years it was only Grendel who enjoyed the bloody feasts now held in Heorot. The Danes dwelt in terror as each of Hrothgar's thanes were slain or were made to be of no more use. Help came to Hrothgar from far lands, but still Grendel pillaged and slew with grisly delight. Heorot sat in ghastly silence; even the skald's voice had been silenced by the unbound battle runes. The Spear-Danes despaired that their king had been abandoned by the Gods.

Across the whale's way in great Geatland, the son of Ecgtheow, brave Beowulf, thrived as the foster son of the good king, Hrethel the One-Eyed. His first winters had been spent with Hrothgar's Spear-Danes after his father's blood feud with the Wulfings sent his family into exile. Hrothgar opened his home to the clanless warrior and his kin. In those years with the Spear-Danes, Ecgtheow's courage and loyalty were proven many times. Hrothgar declared Ecgtheow as shield friend and battle brother and gifted him with the wergild that would end the feud with the Wulfings. His honor regained and wergild in hand, Ecgtheow and Beowulf returned to their homeland.

Alas, honorable Ecgtheow fell in battle soon after his return to Geatland. Fatherless at only seven winters, Fate smiled upon the young Beowulf and made him a prince of the Geats, a foster son of good King Hrethel. From Hrethel came riches, kinship, and, perhaps mightiest of all, the remembered deeds of his father, noble Ecgtheow, thane and kinsman of that noble king.

Hrethel had blood sons whom he loved well. When Fate took Haethcyn's life in a hunting accident at the hand of his own brother, Herebeald, the good king could not master his grief. His misery and pain stole his life breath; Hrethel the One-Eyed died broken-hearted and now mourns in Fensalir with the Allmother.

Hygelac, son of Hrethel, took the wise queen, Hygd, as his wife, and together they ruled the Geats with kindness and goodness, both well loved by their clan. Hygelac, mighty in battle, was blessed by the gods. An enchanted horn he had been given, a *gealdor-gifu*, whose song would call the gods to battle.

Beowulf, Geatish prince and foster brother to Hygelac, became a mighty warrior well known in the North lands. When word came across the whale road of Hrothgars-Bane, Beowulf told his clan of the Danes' generosity and the oaths spoken between the Danish king and his father. Hygelac and Hygd did not hesitate; they urged Beowulf to gather his warriors and bring an end to Grendel's grim feast.

Hrothgar and his queen, wise Wealtheow, welcomed Beowulf and his warriors to the cold hearth of Heorot. Elated they were to see the Geat again and most comforted by the presence of the many swords. Wealtheow had a feast prepared, and the fires and torches were lit in the hall at her behest. The empty cups were filled with honey wine as Wealtheow went forth and offered the first cup to her chieftain, beloved Hrothgar. To Beowulf, she offered the cup of welcome, and with her grateful smile, some cheer returned to the great hall.

But not all were happy to see Beowulf and his warrior band. Unferth, covetous and small minded, a Dane who had yet to raise his sword against Grendel, sulked in silence during the feast. When the honey wine loosened his tongue, he challenged that Geatish prince with a reminder that a rumored rowing match between Beowulf and Breca, a longtime friend, had ended with Beowulf's defeat. A much-worse Fate would befall Beowulf, Unferth predicted, if he challenged the bone grinder, that fiend Grendel.

A silence fell upon Heorot as Beowulf stood to answer Unferth's words.

"Fate will save an uncursed man," Beowulf spoke slowly, "if his strength is steady. For seven days and nights I slipped through the swells of the deep. Dreadful it was, but my dismay was worse when I lost sight of Breca. I finally made the shore and found Breca had reached it first. Still, it was a victory for us both that we survived the abyss."

Unferth simply scowled as the company's mead cups were drained, followed by shouts of "SKÅL!" as Beowulf continued: "My thought when my warriors and I set to the sea and sailed in our ship is that I would toil for the good of your people or battling, fall to Fate within this monster's strong grasp. I am fixed to do a warrior's bold feat."

When they heard these words, Hrothgar and those gathered in his hall that night nearly wept from relief and joy. Filled with hope, the king of the Danes bade his people a good rest, and with a final toast the old king took to his bed, with Wealtheow soon following.

As the Spear-Danes left the hall and sought their slumber, Beowulf prepared for the coming battle with Grendel. The Geat warrior knew that the bone grinder crushed with his bare hands and tore with his gnarled teeth. Ever watchful, Beowulf stripped off his armor and weapons. Stalwart, he felt no fear; his *wyrd* was set as was his purpose.

Across the moor came Grendel, skulking beneath the shadowed cliffs. To Heorot his footsteps led, his intent another grim feast. The fires of fury burned in his fingers when he tore the hinges off the hall doors. He beheld the circle of kinsman sleeping; his eyes shone with his desire for fresh meat.

On the bare floor Beowulf lay, eyes closed but his hearing keen and sharp. Mighty warrior, hero, and prince, he felt when Grendel snatched a fellow Geat; heard the bone snap and knew that skuld was taking that brave warrior to Valhalla. Still as silence, the warriors waited. Beowulf let the bone grinder gorge on the corpse; let him become drunk as he devoured his feast.

The moment when Grendel swallowed the last grim morsel, Beowulf, bare handed, with lightning-fast grip, fastened his hands on the monster's foul flesh. In those hands flowed the *galdr-gifu* of the Aesir; Grendel knew his feasting days in Heorot were finished.

Beowulf, with the bone breaker firmly in his grasp, unleashed his fury. Heorot barely withstood the crashing of timber as benches were broken. Grendel screamed as he struggled; to the moors he must go or else be ripped to pieces by Odin's wolf. The shoulder sinews tore, the limb useless now as the flesh began to rip. Beowulf was relentless; his iron grip never weakened. The meaty arm tore loose, blood flowing into a death pool, and Grendel, determined not to die in the hall of his hated enemy, fled into the dark, leaving his torn limb behind.

When the sky candle rose, Beowulf, his fellow Geats, and the Danes all followed Grendel's bloody trail to a tide pool near the sea. There, they found the waters tangled with the gore that had once been the fiend of Heorot.

Returning to high Heorot, Hrothgar's gratitude was great; his gifts were many to the Geats: a golden standard, helm and mail shirt, jewels, embossed shields, and eight horses with burnished bridles. A banquet was held in Heorot like none that had ever been held before; that ring palace gleamed with pride and joy.

Wealtheow praised good Beowulf as he sat between her sons, surrounded by the other Danish youths. The shadow of Hrothulf lingered nearby, and indeed she saw it. She felt no fear; instead, she remembered the kindness that the Danes had shown to Hrothgar's nephew. That wise queen hoped for more than what she could see.

The Danes and Geats went soon to slumber after the feast was done. Beowulf slept this night in a hero's bed not far from the fires of Hrothgar's Hall. But, in mighty Heorot, where the gruesome arm of Grendel adorned the rafters above the sleeping warriors, the quiet was soon shattered.

Having fled to the moors, his mother he did seek. Shrieking and moaning, Grendel fell into her embrace. She comforted her son as his lifeblood poured out of him; she held him closely to her breast and sang a mother's woe as he died. Her hot tears burned her as they fell.

Silent as a shadow, she came to Heorot. The she-wolf entered the doors and stood staring at the sleeping sentinels. No one and nothing stirred. Her eyes were drawn upward. A shriek of monstrous horror spewed forth from her deformed lips: she had seen her son's arm.

Screaming as she attacked, Grendel's mother swept up a Spear-Dane in her meaty arms. Battle brother to Hrothgar, Aeschere was now a monster's murder. Off she sprinted, past the moors and down to the deep, murky waters of the cursed mere.

The morning brought anguish and horror back to Heorot; Hrothgar mourned his shoulder companion, beloved Aeschere, taken by the hag. Beowulf, grieved and angry, comforted the old king; he would find Grendel's mother and avenge Aeschere, best of warriors.

"I will go and give my life blood in order to end this misery for you, beloved Hrothgar," Beowulf swore. "Should I fall in this battle, be a good king to my companions and send them to my home with your gifts for honorable King Hygelac and Queen Hygd."

Off went brave Beowulf with the Spear-Danes and Geats in company. As they rode into the wild lands, Hrothgar told the tale of the two creatures.

"These have wandered in exile and belong to no clan. They guard the wolf lairs, the deep fens, the wind-beaten lands. Near to where the mountain floods rattle and flow into an underground stream, where no creature, not even the pursued stag with the hounds at his heels, dare enter, that is their lair."

"Grieve no more, wise Hrothgar," Beowulf said. "Arise and ride with me. Today, the Danes will be avenged."

It was not long after crossing a sharp ravine that the company came to a cliff. There, they found brave Aeschere's severed head. The river here had a strong current and seethed with shadowy movement. Wild beasts and worms, serpents, and mere dragons, they all twisted within the water. Beowulf put on his armor and, with his bow, quickly slew one of the beasts. It was but one of many.

As the hero prepared to enter the murky waters, Unferth quickly stepped forward, with Hrunting, a powerful sword, in his hand. A mighty weapon, Hrunting was from an ancient treasure, its iron edge poison to its enemy. Hrunting had never failed in battle, and now Unferth, once Beowulf's challenger, offered the blade in friendship. Beowulf took the sword and nodded to Unferth in silent thanks.

Eager for the coming battle, Beowulf made his way swiftly down into the underground stream. Many monsters he slew as he sought the she-wolf in the depths. As the water grew ever deeper, from the depths she came. Grendel's mother struck hard, clutching the ring prince in a mighty grip. Her claws and teeth tore at Beowulf, but the mail shirt held fast. Deeper they sank, a mighty struggle with the mere woman. As the battle swirled the waters, more monsters came and lashed Beowulf's flesh with twisted tentacle and sharp fin.

Nearly overcome, Beowulf's battle fury belched forth as he drew Hrunting, that mighty blade. As he turned to stab the hag, he spied within the gloom a roofed hall beneath them; it shone bright and gleamed with charmed fire. Down he pushed, swimming with all his might, gripping Hrunting tightly. On his heels came the hag.

A Giant's hall, filled with sweet air and treasures from times forgotten; this was where Beowulf or Grendel's mother must meet their doom. Hrunting in hand, Beowulf swung the blade and felt it slam against the hag's head. Biteless, the blade bounced back; the mere woman could not be harmed by its magic.

Nearby lay a Giant's sword, jeweled and gleaming in the light. Beowulf leapt toward it as the she-wolf again seized him. Crazed she was and her strength great; her claws ripped and tore in a frenzy. Charmed, the war hero's armor held fast; she drew no blood from him. Seizing his moment, grasping the Giant's blade, Beowulf smote the fiend woman hard.

Bones broke and blood flowed as Grendel's mother fell to the stone. She trembled and convulsed, gurgling curses upon Beowulf as she died. Beowulf felt no remorse or regret for her slaying; that wergild now paid full in blood. Near her lay Grendel, one-armed, his face contorted from his death struggle. With the Giant's blade, Beowulf took the grinder's head, a gift for Hrothgar.

Far above, the Danes and Geats watched as the waters surged and filled with gore. They feared that mighty Beowulf had fallen, that the hag had been his doom. The warriors sat and stared silently at the dark water. As they despaired, the head of the ring prince emerged from the swirling currents. With the Giant's sword in one hand and the head of Grendel in the other, Beowulf hailed his companions with news of his victory. As he told the tale and held the sword aloft, the blade turned to ice, shriveled, and melted as they all watched in awe. With praise to the gods and with Grendel's head upon a spear, the victorious company journeyed back to golden Heorot.

The celebration of Beowulf's victory over Grendel's mother lasted for many days. Heorot was truly a place of joy and celebration. Hrothgar was generous with his gifts; Beowulf was gracious in his acceptance. The time was nigh, though, for the Geats to return to their own ring giver back across the whale road. It was a sad farewell, yet many oaths of friendship were spoken. Beowulf had triumphed. It was time to go home.

More than fifty years pass . . .

In a cave on the hill, a hoard there was, deep within a dark hollow. Guarded by the fire breather, only a sheer passage led to the mighty treasure. None dared go there; none dared to disturb the long sleep of the worm.

Yet, a single goblet, a small cup of gold from this mighty hoard, became Beowulf's bane. Stolen by a fool who entered the lair while the worm was away, the cup was immediately missed by the dragon upon his return. Enraged, the dragon could smell the thief and swore to take his vengeance. Belching fire and smoke, the dragon tracked the thief to his home and laid waste to it. The surrounding countryside fared no better; cattle and sheep burned, and every building destroyed.

Good King Beowulf soon heard of the worm's rampage. Aged and wise, he knew that the dragon's revenge had to be stopped. Ordering a shield of iron to be crafted for him, the old king prepared for dragon battle. He refused a large war band, choosing instead eleven battle brothers, among them Wiglaf, Weohstan's son.

To the cave and the dark hollow they went, scaling the passage down into the dragon's lair. Halting at the threshold, Beowulf spoke to his companions: "I am eager to battle this winged terror and see which of us is the better. Lo, this is not your battle, my brothers, so here you must await my return."

To the stone arches the aged king went, striding mightily as he once did in his youth. Sword in hand and iron shield raised, Beowulf let loose his war cry to the dragon. In answer, the dragon's breath spewed forth, hot and boiling. Coiling, the worm was still in shadow, but then it emerged, his horned head wreathed in flame.

Beowulf brandished his sword and met the mighty beast stride for stride. The world trembled as they clashed and smote. Their battle was mighty; cries of anguish and roars of anger emerged from the smoky cave. The companions waited, troubled at the signs, fearing their leader was lost. As flame and heat exploded from the shadows, the warriors fled from the blast.

Wiglaf, thane and kinsman of Beowulf, stood fast. That warrior mustered his courage from memories of his king's generosity. Armor, weapons, food, and a bed in the king's hall were all gifted to Wiglaf by the aged king. To his fleeing companions Wiglaf cried out, "Oaths you spoke as you accepted the many gifts from Beowulf in his great hall! Our lord has great need of us now! Alone he faces the dragon, wounded and bleeding; his sword has failed him. Come! Find your courage! I, for one, will not let him die alone."

Into the hot smoke Wiglaf went, Weohstan's son, much-loved warrior. He found Beowulf with his sword in hand, his shield raised as he waited for the dragon's next attack.

"Mighty you were when you vanquished the Grendels from Hrothgar's hall," Wiglaf said as he joined his king. "You are mighty now, great king, but you need not meet this monster alone. I will stand with you."

As Wiglaf's words finished, the dragon, freshly enraged, emerged and advanced upon the king and thane. Battle ensued again as flames devoured Wiglaf's wooden shield. Naegling, heirloom of Beowulf's clan, sword of iron, met the dragon's scales with a mighty stroke. The blade failed then; cracked and bent, both sword and Beowulf fell.

Three duels and three strokes; the end was near. Hot and grim with war, the worm seized Beowulf's throat in its mouth. Blood and venom burst; Beowulf gasped as he writhed. A dagger there was, swift and sharp, still sheathed to Beowulf's side. This he drew and thrust upward into the worm's belly, delivering a death blow to the beast.

With little strength left, the good king lay still. Wiglaf removed Beowulf's helmet and washed the grave wound. Already it was swollen, and soon it began to burn.

"If I had a son, today I would give him my armor," Beowulf spoke. "For fifty winters, I have kept my people safe and tried to always be a good king. Wiglaf, my brave warrior, the worm is dead, and I am dying. I would gaze upon the hoard that he so jealously guarded. I would see my doom in full before I depart this world."

Wiglaf understood and entered the worm's treasure chamber. He filled the iron shield with jewels and gold. These he brought to where Beowulf lay dying.

"Ah, good Wiglaf, it fills me with great pride to gaze upon these jewels," Beowulf gasped, "and it is my wish that these should go to our people. The dragon is dead; you need not fear his wrath."

"It will be done, Beowulf," Wiglaf promised.

"Build me a mound," the old king whispered, "atop the Whale-Rising, and call it Beowulf's Barrow."

"Yes," Wiglaf said softly.

"Take this," Beowulf smiled and removed the golden torque from his neck. "You are the last of our kin. Wear it well."

As his last breath left his body, the companions, the cowards who had fled, gathered closely around. They gazed upon their king and wept.

Wiglaf taunted them, "What is life without honor?"

The unfaithful had nothing to say.

A barrow they built in ten days and filled it with rings and jewels. They lit the fires for the pyre and dressed Beowulf in his finest armor. The sailors from afar could see Beowulf's Barrow as the sons of the twelve chieftains rode 'round. A woman of woe, standing alone with her hair bound in mourning, sang her despair. Gone was good Beowulf! Departed is our kind king! Well loved, generous, and wise, Beowulf is gone to Valhalla, home of the brave.

three

IN FATE'S FOOTSTEPS: HOW THE ORACLE WORKS

The universal appeal of the *Beowulf* poem stems from the primal quality of the tale itself, which deals with the struggle to overcome obstacles, the heroism, and a continuing search for a fulfilled and fulfilling life. The adventures and heroic deeds of the warriors bound together in fellowship, along with the adversaries they encounter, both human and magical, make their paths ones that affect everyone who reads about them.

The characters of the northern myths are far more than just men and women; they are also archetypes that embody many of the most important characteristics of the human experience. It is thus possible to identify closely with each character from the stories and to journey with them—learning from their deep fount of wisdom and growing in the process. In this way we learn to know and understand our own inner Heroes, the strong and powerful persona that hides beneath our external selves. *The Beowulf Oracle* is more than just a tool for exploring the inner self—it is also a way of finding answers to the questions and issues that we encounter daily. As such, it is both a personal tool for exploration and a powerful oracle to help in making decisions.

Guided by one of the three Norns, holders of fate in northern mythology, we travel from Midworld to one of the Nine Realms, accompanied by one or other of the characters who inhabit the ancient world of the poem. Along the way, we discover new and powerful truths about ourselves, drawing upon a deep pool of wisdom that stretches back to a time when the world was a simpler place. Here, answers tended to be more black and white (though no easier for that), a wisdom that strikes to the heart of the problem.

These individual encounters bring guidance by challenging us to take a deeper look at the circumstances of whatever issue we bring to the oracle. In this way we discover new ways to overcome obstacles, find new paths, or reinterpret already-occurring events in an empowering way, after which we return to the Norns for a final weaving of wonder and fate.

The deeper ways between the worlds are not lost to us, any more than the great heroes and heroines of those older times. We can still journey to meet them whenever we wish, and find council, wisdom, and support when it is most needed. *The Beowulf Oracle* was devised for exactly this purpose and is based on the principle that both the places and people it describes possess a reality that can be accessed in vision and meditation, and through imagery. They also serve as jumping-off places for those who seek to explore their own journey, and to discover more about the path upon which they have already set out or that they will soon follow.

The individual characters act in two ways, according to our need and preference: as **Companions** on your journey to find your wyrd or fate. They can be Heroes, walking at your side and guiding your steps along the way, offering advice and wisdom that can be acquired either through meditation or from the brief statements to be found for each card in this book. Or they can act as Challengers, who require of you that you look for deeper meanings to your journey and to the questions you may be holding (not always spoken or even acknowledged) along the way. Three additional cards, the Norns, represent aspects of fate from past, present, or future, whose influence will have a powerful effect on your journey. You will be brought by your companion to one of the Nine Realms, each of which brings its own oracular meaning, and last of all you return to the Norns for a powerful "weaving" of wyrd and wisdom. The combination of these creates your personal oracle.

Before you start using *The Beowulf Oracle*, we suggest you take time to look at each image carefully, noting expressions, setting, and any other details. Is there one character you feel more drawn to than the rest? Would you want that person as a Hero or a Challenger? Would you like them to be your friend? Now look at the faces of the Norns. For which one do you feel a special sympathy? Which is the most fearful?

Now turn to the book and read the text concerning the characters and places. Once you feel that you know something about each person, you are ready to begin.

Beowulf's Journey

The premise of *The Beowulf Oracle* is simple. Within the box you will find a set of twenty cards, each one bearing a portrait of one of the characters and objects from the poem. Together they represent an understanding of countless human issues that you are likely to encounter in your life.

With these you will also find three extra cards: the Norns. These are the northern depiction of the Fates, who oversee, *but do not control*, the destiny of those who undertake the journeys. Together, they represent Past, Present, and Future and will offer guidance to the direction of your journey, as well as adding a significant weaving of fate into the answers the oracle provides.

In addition, you will find a map of Yggdrasil, the World Tree p. 129, including the Nine Realms, which have acquired their own archetypal meaning and have come to embody truths and situations that we all experience at one time or another. These have three layers of meaning, according to the category of your question: Life (general), Love (relationships), and Work. All paths begin and end at Midgard, which represents the world we ourselves inhabit, and from which we set forth and to which we return. A combination of the messages presented by these cards creates the oracle.

Making a Reading

The oracle begins and ends with the Norns, the holders of fate and the keepers of wyrd or destiny for all men and women in the ancient Norse world. Present your question to them, for it is they who initiate your journey in search of an answer, guiding you to choose your companion(s), drawn from the poem of *Beowulf* and illustrated on the card deck that accompanies this book, who will in turn point you to the realm you need to visit for your concluding oracle.

Here, then, are the simple instructions to make a reading from the oracle.

1: Finding Your Question and Your Wyrd

Coming up with the right question and phrasing it correctly is an art in itself. You may think you know the issue you want to address—and you probably do—but how to phrase it? The simpler the question, the more direct the answer you will receive. Avoid yes/no, either/or questions, since these tend to muddy the waters and give you indecisive answers. Ones beginning with "Should I . . ." mean you have abandoned responsibility for your actions and handed them over to the oracle. Thus, instead of asking, for example, "Should I move in with Mike?," it would be better to ask: "What qualities does Mike have that would make him an ideal partner?," for instance. Some good formats are the following:

> What is the likely consequence if . . . ?
> Please show me how I might . . .
> Please guide me . . .
> Help me to see clearly . . .
> Help me to move forward . . .

All of these will help you to get clearer answers.

2: Visiting the Norns

In chapter 5 you will find a brief ceremony that brings added depths to the discovery of your wyrd. Here we give just a simple beginning.

Once you have your question clear in your mind, take the three Norn cards out of the deck and mix them up, sight unseen, and lay them facedown. Thinking of your question, turn over one of the cards. Either silently or aloud, say: *I come before you with a question, in search of my wyrd.* Whichever Norn you have chosen will decide the next stage of your journey, focusing either on

The Past, (Urd, meaning "What Once Was")

The Present, (Verdandi, meaning "What Is Coming into Being")

The Future (Skuld, meaning "What Shall Be").

This lets you know where you should be seeking an answer. Is the truth you seek hidden in the past, does it lurk behind the outward form of the present, or is it awaiting you still in future time? Be aware of the wisdom of the Norns who seek to place your intent in the right place. Perhaps in your ears you will hear the Norn speaking: *Go in search of a Companion or a Hero, a Challenger, or both. Seek their wisdom in the time we have shown you. Follow where they lead to one of the Nine Realms, and on your return I will rede you your wyrd.*

The presence of the Norns runs as a thread of wisdom throughout your journey. The powerful Weavings of the Norns, which follow the specific messages for each character and realm in chapter 4, augment and develop the answers you seek. They complete the reading of the wyrd.

3: Choosing a Companion

Now it is time to choose a Companion from the main deck. This will be one of the characters or objects from the poem. You should spend a little time with these before you begin, studying the image and then reading the brief account of this character in the entry for the card to be found in chapter 4. Each character may act as Hero or Challenger, or even, perhaps, as both. Each bears a message for whichever aspect you choose. The Hero is your ally who will lead you to your destination in the Nine Worlds; as Challenger they may encourage you to ask questions of yourself, seeking out the true reason for your journey, which you may not always realize at first. You may choose either aspect or allow your companion to act as both. You may not think that you want to take Grendel or Grendel's mother with you on any journey, but remember these are archetypal forces whose understanding of human nature is far greater than our own. Whichever companion you choose will have something to offer you.

Here are the two ways of choosing your Companion:

(1) Select a card randomly, allowing the oracle to decide for you, or according to your feeling and intuition, having studied the cards and read the information provided below each picture in this book. This will help you understand which character is best suited to help you in this particular journey.

(2) Turn to chapter 5, where you will find a specifically designed spread, Heorot Spread, which will help you choose a Hero or Challenger (or both) according to your own place at the Table of the Geats.

At this point you may choose to read the message brought to you by the card, either as hero or challenger or both. Two brief kennings will be found underneath these longer statements. These are the Weaving of the Norns, bringing a deeper meaning to the response. They refer both to Hero and Challenger and add an important strand to the reading.

4: Finding Your Way in the Nine Realms

Now shuffle the pack and, having pulled a card at random, let it fall where it will onto the tabletop or other flat surface (turn it faceup if it falls otherwise). Notice which way the card is pointing. Is the head of the figure or object pointing up or down, to the left or right, or at an angle? This tells you in which direction, and to which of the Nine Realms, you will be journeying.

Now consult the diagram on p. 129. There you will see an image of Yggdrasil, the World Tree, in whose roots and branches the nine sacred realms are lodged. At the center lies Midgard, this world, where all journeys begin and end. Whichever one is nearest to the direction where your card fell is where your journey leads.

Each of the Nine Realms has a different association, and each one carries a message for you that is part of your oracle. The realms, and the qualities they represent, are

ALFHEIM	LUCK AND DESTINY
ASGARD	TRUTH AND HONOR
JOTUNHEIM	STRENGTH AND WISDOM
MUSPELHEIM	VISION AND CREATION
NEIFLHEIM	LOSS AND TRANSFORMATION
NIDVELLIR	TREASURE AND DREAM
SVARTHEIM	POWER AND CUNNING
VALHALLA	REST AND ACHIEVEMENT
VANAHEIM	HIDDEN MEMORY AND MAGIC

You will find full accounts, and readings for each, following the Companion cards, in chapter 4.

5: Reading Your Oracle

Turn to the text for each card (chapter 4), which provide answers according to which aspect of your companion you have chosen: Hero or Challenger. If you have chosen your companion to act as *both* Hero and Challenger, read both messages.

Now read the appropriate message attached to the realm you have journeyed to, followed by the Weavings of the Norns from the Hero or Challenger cards, including the wyrd sayings or the kennings, which you will find after the messages from the realms, which are an important part of the reading.

This is your wyrd.

You may hear it in the voice of the Norn, who redes your wyrd to you. You should thank she who was your guide and contemplate the wisdom that was brought to you through her response.

If you have questions that do not fit any of the categories, or if you wish to extend and deepen the reading, it is suggested that you meditate with the cards, holding each one in your hands and allowing them to speak to you. They may promote a dialogue, speaking directly to you, or you might ask their opinion about your issue. You are at liberty to engage with any of the characters, places, or Norns. Always consider what comes to your mind—or your lips; it could be real gold. In addition, there are some specific runic interpretations for each of the Companion cards, which you will find in chapter 5. These can be used to further augment or deepen the reading.

The reading thus follows this pattern:

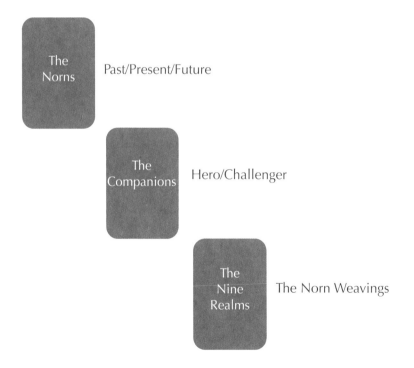

The Norns — Past/Present/Future

The Companions — Hero/Challenger

The Nine Realms — The Norn Weavings

Here is a sample reading made with *The Beowulf Oracle*.

Question: Mary, a widow, was having trouble relating to her son, now a twenty-year-old, who had yet to fulfill her hopes for him. She asked the oracle how she could best help him "find his future."

She drew the Norn Urd, who pointed her toward the past. She was surprised by this, since she had expected present or future but agreed to proceed.

She drew Beowulf himself, as the best protector and source of strength she could think of, and chose him as Hero. She read his message.

I stand at your shoulder and my shield covers you against harm. I walk before you on every road you take, and I speak only truth concerning the choices to be made. I touch the darkness and the light with equal strength, and my sight shows the way forward into either place. I have fought many monsters and I know their names and faces. I will speak to your deepest ancestors and call upon them for truth and guidance. I will protect you against all comers and show you the way to the wisdom you seek.

Thus encouraged, she let the card fall. It pointed to Neifleheim, which referenced loss, transformation, and kinship. She read the message as follows:

Much may be hidden before it is revealed. In this realm, many choices are set before you. This is a place of purification, where old patterns and stories are purged to make way for new. Those who come here seek restoration and vitality. They are offered it when they are willing to see that old patterns must be let go of, and that new friendships may be made. The strength of kinship is important to all who seek progress. Old ways are not always best. Children must grow and become men or women. Old links must be undone.

Mary was deeply moved by this. She saw it an indication that she had been trying too hard to hold on to her son and to guide his steps rather than setting him free to find his own way.

She now turned back to the entry for Beowulf and read the Hero message from "The Weaving of the Norns":

> Devoted to clan and to kindred, stand forthright!
> Ready to reckon with threat from afar.
> Greet now the hero who shields your dear homestead.

Pledge with the welcome cup he who makes safe.
Grateful to guest friend, at your own hearth fire,
Seat him with honour; give him your best!

In this Mary saw both herself *and* her son. She was very determined to protect and guide him, even though she now believed she must give him freedom to grow. She also wanted to celebrate him, as the Weaving suggested. But she also saw that he was equally determined to care for her, and that the mutual love of parent and child was a stronger bond between them than seeking to control his destiny. The Norn, who knew more of this subject than any, had led her to the best understanding of her own deeper wish. By looking to the past, she was able to see her way to the future.

We heard later than she had kept to her realization, and that not only had her son's career taken off, but he had begun to be much more caring of her than in previous time.

four

THE CARDS AND THEIR MEANINGS

(THE COMPANIONS, HEROES, AND CHALLENGERS)

The Norns

Urd
Verdandi
Skuld

The Companions

Beowulf
King Hrothgar
Queen Wealtheow
Grendel
Grendel's Mother
The Dragon
Unferth
Breca
King Hrethel
Shield Sheafson

Hygelac
Ecgtheow
Hrothulf
Hrethric & Hrothmund
Hygd
Wiglaf
Hrunting
The Stolen Cup
The Unfaithful
The Wailing Widow

THE NORNS

We begin with the Norns, who hold the threads of our wyrd or fate in their hands. Their very names tell us their role in our journey. They ask us to consider whether our journey will take us to the past, the present, or the future, in each of which may lie answers to the issues we bring. They also offer us wisdom concerning the aspects of our daily lives to which we may orient our questions: Life, Love, or Work. The Weaving of the Norns, found in the entries for each of the Companion cards, and the Wyrd Sayings, which follow each of the Nine Realms, form an important part of your wyrd. Here, the Norns bring their own focus to the issue presented by the reader.

According to the *Prose Edda*, compiled by Snorri Sturluson during the twelfth and thirteenth centuries, which is one of the principal sources for Norse mythology, we find the following:

> *A fair hall stands there, under the great ash by a mighty well. And out of that place come three women, who are called thus: Urd, Verdandi, and Skuld. These determine the period of men's live. We call them the Norns. . . . [They] come to each child that is born, to appoint its life, and they are of the race of the Gods. . . . It is further said that these Norns, who dwell by the well, take water daily from it, together with clay that they find around the well. This they sprinkle over the Ash, so that its limbs shall neither wither nor rot. The water is so holy that all things that fall into it become as white as the film within an eggshell. It is said:*

An ash stands there.
It is called Yggdrasil.
A high tree sprinkled
With clay white as snow.
Thence comes the dew
That fall in the dale each day,
So that it stands ever green
Above Urd's Well.

This paints a clear picture: the great tree, with the well at its foot, guarded by the three wise women. What better place to come in search of answers to the trials and tribulations of living? Who better to find the truth about our needs and goals than the Norns, the holders of the threads of fate?

However, we should be aware that sometimes the Norns can be tricky, as we can see in this story from the twelfth-century Danish protohistorian Saxo Grammaticus, which tells a story about the Danish king Fridleif, who took his three-year-old son Olaf to pray to "three maidens sitting on three seats":

'The ancients were wont to consult the oracles of the Fates concerning the destinies of their children. In this way Fridleif desired to search into the fate of his son Olaf, and, after solemnly offering up his vows, he went to the house of the gods in entreaty, where, looking into the chapel, he saw three maidens, sitting on three seats. The first of them was of a benignant temper and bestowed upon the boy abundant beauty and ample store of favor in the eyes of men. The second granted him the gift of surpassing generosity. But the third (a woman of more mischievous temper and malignant disposition, scorning the unanimous kindness of her sisters, and likewise wishing to mar their gifts) marked the future character of the boy with the slur of niggardliness. Thus, the benefits of the others were spoilt by the poison of a lamentable doom, and hence, by virtue of the twofold nature of these gifts, Olaf got his surname from the meanness that was mingled with his bounty. So, it came about that this blemish that found its way into the gift marred the whole sweetness of its first blessing. (Book 6 of Saxo Grammaticus, *Gesta Danorum, The Danish History*)

URD

Meaning "What Once Was" (Old Norse "Urðr"),
she represents the past. She is the guardian
of a sacred well, the waters of which bring healing
and, when mixed with the clay that surrounds the well,
keep the great World Tree alive.

VERDANDI

Meaning "What Is Coming into Being"
(Old Norse "Verðandi"), she represents the present.
She holds the vessel containing some of
Water of Fate.

SKULD

Meaning "What Shall Be" (Old Norse "Skuld"),
she represents the future. She is also a Valkyrie,
one of the women who ride in a host above
battlefields, judging the lives of the fallen and taking
the spirits of those deemed worthy to Valhalla.

RUNE MAGIC

Each of the Companions is designated by a rune, part of the ancient Futhark alphabet of the Norse world. These have complex meanings of their own, and we have attributed those that seem most appropriate to each character or object. You will find these hidden or openly revealed in each picture. In chapter 5 you will find some more suggestions how to work with these.

Here is a list:

BEOWULF—TIWAZ

HROTHGAR—ANSUZ

GRENDEL—HAGALAZ

GRENDEL'S MOTHER—OTHALA

THE DRAGON—KENAZ

WEALTHEOW—URUZ

ᚢ

UNFERTH—THURISAZ

ᚦ

WIGLAF—EHWAZ

ᛖ

BRECA—MANNAZ

ᛗ

HRETHEL—ALGIZ

ᛉ

SHIELD SHEAFSON—FEHU

ᚠ

HYGELAC—GEBO

ᚷ

ECGTHEOW—NAUTHIZ

ᚾ

HYGD—JERA

ᛃ

HROTHULF—ISA

ᛁ

HRETHRIC AND
HROTHMUND—WUNJO

ᚹ

HRUNTING—SOWILO

ᛋ

THE STOLEN CUP—INGUZ

ᛜ

THE UNFAITHFUL—PERTHRO

ᛈ

WAILING WIDOW—BERKANO

ᛒ

BEOWULF

The protagonist of the epic,
Beowulf is a Geatish hero who fights the
monster Grendel, Grendel's mother,
and a fire-breathing dragon. In his youth,
he personifies all the finest values
of the heroic culture. In his old age,
he proves a wise and effective ruler.

My thought when my warriors and I
set to the sea and sailed in our ship,
is that I would toil for the good of your people
in full, or battling fall to Fate
within the monster's strong grasp. I am fixed to do
a warrior's bold feat, or finish the days
of my life here in the hall of a kin.

AS HERO

I stand at your shoulder and my shield covers you against harm. I walk before you on every road you take, and I speak only truth concerning the choices to be made. I touch the darkness and the light with equal strength, and my sight shows the way forward into either place. I have fought many monsters and I know their names and faces. I will speak to your deepest ancestors and call upon them for truth and guidance. I will protect you against all comers and show you the way to the wisdom you seek.

AS CHALLENGER

I call upon you to question your motive in beginning this journey. What is your real need? Have you undertaken this from a place of truth or for a desire to obtain power? Will your steps falter upon the way, or will you continue forward in the face of all perils? Dark places may lie in wait for you, but you must know that I will guide and protect you as well as challenging your every step upon the way. Will you listen to me or will you go forward as your own will requires? Are you foolish or wise? Ask yourself this question before you set forth. Listen only to the truth as you know it.

THE WEAVING OF THE NORNS

HERO

Devoted to clan and to kindred, stand forthright!
Ready to reckon with threat from afar.
Greet now the hero who shields your dear homestead.
Pledge with the welcome cup he who makes safe.
Grateful to guest friend, at your own hearth fire,
Seat him with honor, give him your best!

CHALLENGER

Pride blights good deeds like rust on a sword blade.
Though keen be the vision, set arrogance aside:
When deeds gild the giver more bright than the taker,
Trust cannot flourish, faith decks but the self.
Grasp the hard challenge with strength and with cunning,
Truth be your helmet, and wise wyrd your shield.

2

HROTHGAR

ᚠ

A king of the Danes, Hrothgar enjoys military
success and prosperity until Grendel terrorizes
his realm. A wise and aged ruler, Hrothgar
represents a different kind of leadership from that
exhibited by the youthful warrior Beowulf.
He is a father figure to Beowulf and a model for the
kind of king that Beowulf becomes.

Hrothgar was granted a great sea victory,
clear distinction in combat, so that a clan
followed fondly till his thanes had grown
to a large band of young men.

AS HERO

I welcome you to my great hall and stand ready to reward your brave deeds. I will provide the weapons, armor, and any other tool that you need to conquer and vanquish what troubles you. I come from a long line of good kings who seek only to provide the best for their clan and kindred. There is a shadow of sadness behind me, but the strength of my great hall holds the shadows at bay. I have fought in many battles, both on land and on the great whale road. I am old now, but in my youth I was strong and keen with a sword. I am closer to the place of the ancestors than I am to the world of the living.

AS CHALLENGER

Look now to the purpose you hold for this journey. Will you rise to the moment and be strengthened by the oracle, or will you cower before the issues that arise and hide your head beneath the waters of dream? Many come before me with questions and offers of service, but not all are truthful. Only by looking into the depths of your intention can you find the answers you seek. Do not run and do not hide: the wheel of time turns whatever you do. As the one who walks at your side, I will guide you to the place of truth and courage.

THE WEAVING OF THE NORNS

HERO

Strong once, in battle proven, now in need;
Giver of arm rings, beloved of your clan.
Who will come now to shelter the homestead?
Who will lift threat from the shadowing hearthstone?
Welcome the guest friend who sets hand to help you,
Open gates gladly, with kingly toast pledged,
Bring into kinship with richest reward.

CHALLENGER

False are the gifts, words they speak double,
False friends speak failure, to turn you aside.
Let not these doubts cloud your judgment or valor,
Hold to your purpose, keep faith with your wyrd.
Break from doubt's prison, to vanquish and conquer,
Faith bright and focused to win to your end.

3

WEALTHEOW

Hrothgar's wife, the gracious queen
of the Danes. Wealtheow sees and knows much;
her sturdy strength holds Heorot together as
Hrothgar despairs from Grendel's relentless
attacks. When Beowulf and his companions
arrive, Wealtheow welcomes them with
a hero's toast. She sees Beowulf as a symbol
of hope for the future of Heorot
and for her two young sons.

Went Wealtheow forth, queen of Hrothgar, mindful of manners,
gold adorned, hailed the heroes in the hall;
first, to the guardian of the East Danes' homeland
she gave to her lord a drink,
beloved chieftain

AS HERO

I have seen much in my lifetime and learned from it wisdom that may guide others. As I guide my husband the king and my children, and as I watch over the mead hall of Heorot, so may I guide your steps upon the way. As Queen and Mother, I keep watch and lend my strength to those in need. Come sit at my table in the hall and drink deeply of my wisdom. Sit by my side and speak your deepest thoughts into my ear. Follow where I lead and learn to grow strong by calling upon your own wisdom. Match for match, let us talk and understand that not all paths lead to the same place; not all goals are to be sought.

AS CHALLENGER

My wisdom is grounded in the earth on which all walk. I will not praise or applaud you, but I will challenge your most fundamental notions. How will you respond? Will you bypass my knowledge, which sees further and more deeply than you may know? How will you come to terms with matters of which you thought you had knowledge, but now it seems you do not? Come, test yourself against the harshness of reality. Do not allow your dreams to overwhelm you. Lean from those who are heroes to be a hero for yourself.

THE WEAVING OF THE NORNS

HERO

Far sight comes keenest from kindlers of hearth fire,
Home is a stronghold, a gift to all kin.
Learn to see shadows of wyrd when they're forming,
As mother sees child growing fast to a man.
Ponder the vision, search deeply the knowledge,
Choose well with cunning the paths of your span.

CHALLENGER

Unfast the roof ties, uncaring the keeper,
Who spins, weaving cloaks for herself to behold.
Orphaning guests with the whey milk of welcome,
Cold is the hearth, where the guest cup cheers not.
Seek for the strength of the ancestral fires,
Bathe in the blessing that keeps your life warm.

GRENDEL

ᚾ

A monstrous creature guilty of murder,
Grendel is exiled from his clan.
Envious of the joy that he observes in Heorot,
Grendel brings misery and death by preying on
Hrothgar's warriors as they sleep in the king's mead
hall. His ruthless and miserable existence is part of
the retribution exacted for his heinous crimes.
Grendel fits solidly within the ethos of
vengeance that governs the world of Beowulf
as both perpetrator and prey.

The monster relished his savage war
On the Danes, keeping the bloody feud
Alive, seeking no peace, offering
No truce, accepting no settlement, no price
In gold or land, and paying the living
For one crime only with another. No one
Waited for reparation from his plundering claws:
That shadow of death hunted in the darkness,
Stalked Hrothgar's warriors.

AS HERO

Those who seek me will find me a grim companion. Many have come to me with outstretched hands, begging for answers. Many have I sent back to think again of their reasons for coming. Those I help will know me well and will follow where I lead. I may clear all obstacles before you, but I may myself become a force who must be met with and answered before any passing can occur. Look then with care upon the road you have chosen. Which of the Nine Worlds do you truly seek?

AS CHALLENGER

You may feel you are strong and brave enough to overcome the fears and concerns that dog your path, but there are those who are stronger and adversaries more cunning than you expect. I shall challenge them all, but I challenge you also to answer these questions: What has brought me to this point on my journey? What choices have I not seen that might have brought me where I needed to be? Is the need I bring to this place enough to bear me up and carry me to victory? Be careful not to allow your innermost fears to hold you back. Only with strength and fortitude can you overcome the trials of your life.

THE WEAVING OF THE NORNS

HERO

Harsh the berserker who, shrouded in darkness,
Wields the raw power from depth of the earth.
Harness him firmly, temper his rawness,
Meld lead with iron, to couple its worth.
Watch the flames' color, when white heat is fiercest,
Strike with the courage of spear's mighty force.

CHALLENGER

Merciless stripper of flesh from bare bone,
Destroyer of settlements, bane of fair home.
Courage be swiftest, arm be strongest,
Show your worth fastest to master this harm.
Strike a truce quickest, this warrior enlist,
Together in honor, unlock earth's dark kist

GRENDEL'S MOTHER

An unnamed swamp hag, Grendel's mother
seems to possess even fewer human
qualities than Grendel, although her terrorization
of Heorot is explained by her desire for vengeance
for the death of her son—a human motivation.
Here she watches over the great cauldron of life,
upon which are depicted many facets
of human activity.

She'd brooded on her loss,
misery had brewed in her heart,
that female horror, Grendel's mother,
living in the murky cold lake
Assigned her since her son
had killed his only brother,
slain his father's son
With an angry sword.

AS HERO

I am a mother who loves her clan and kindred with deep, passionate devotion. Exiled because of my child's treacherous kin slaying, I brood in the dark waters of doubt, fear, and anger. I trust precious few and precious little, but once I swear my oath of kinship, I am relentless in my duties as mother and protector. Seek me if you can muster the courage to stare into the deep abyss. My home is the Giants' castle, and in my house are many treasures that I keep close and well.

AS CHALLENGER

To you I say: What life challenge brought you here? How will you seek to find a solution? Will you look to the times that are gone, to the ancestors perhaps? Or will you cast your eyes upon the future, looking for dangers to come rather than those that are current? Whichever of these paths you chose, or are chosen for you, remember that all life is lived in layers, and that when one layer is peeled away, another is revealed—until you reach the last layer of all, where time no longer moves and you are face to face with your truth.

THE WEAVING OF THE NORNS

HERO

Hideous of aspect, the womb of outpouring,
The birther of brave ones, who leap to the fray:
Guardian of Giant holm, treasures bestowing,
Bringer of mystery, savager of prey.
Cling to the cauldron of life and redemption,
When judgment and vengeance are stirred among men.

CHALLENGER

If loss be your keeper, revenge be your reaper,
You hasten your wyrd to the stretch of your thread;
The one who destroys to make good his insulting,
Unweaves his own making in wreckage of dread.
Temper the conflict, let truce be your master,
Peace weaver be known as among your own kin.

6

THE DRAGON

An ancient, powerful serpent,
the dragon guards a horde of treasure in a
hidden mound. Beowulf's fight with the dragon
constitutes the third and final part of the epic.

In the cave on the hill a hoard it held,
Deep within the dark hollow.
A sheer passage accessed it,
strange and masked to mortals.

AS HERO

Cunning is my name. I guard the deep treasures and seek to find yet more. I can lead you to discover your own inner riches, but I may well seek to hold them to ransom while you search deeper for more. Be aware also that I am a guardian. I may lie before the doorway that admits you to great wonder and wealth. I may also open that door to you and usher you inside. Also, I cling to the pillar of destiny, watchful and waiting for all who come. Will you trust me or not?

AS CHALLENGER

I lie before you, and my serpentine coils enfold all the knowledge you require to uncover the meaning you seek. Will you face me and answer these questions: Where are you bound on your life journey? Is there one that will accompany you amongst those who live in the outer world of Midgard? How will finding this answer help you? Is there a decision you must make that you have not the courage to own? If you answer these, I will unlock my coils and send you on your way. Otherwise there may be no purpose to your journey.

THE WEAVING OF THE NORNS

HERO

Chance is the shape-shifter, travail the hammer.
Go through the world on the anvil of change.
None can climb higher or reach the advantage,
Unless they seize courage and shed their own skin.
Treasures be greater, possessions the richer,
Who strives and succeeds with the aid of a friend.

CHALLENGER

Let he who stores treasures deep in a casket,
Hold fast, and beware of the thief who breaks in.
Envy and jealousy twine fast to steal it,
Where heart is locked tight against sharing or gift.
Call on the forebears, to imbue you with wisdom,
With guarding and purpose, hold fast to your key.

7

UNFERTH

ᚦ

Unferth is a thane of Hrothgar, and one
of the few men to have survived Grendel's attacks
upon Heorot and the Danes. Unferth's faith and
courage are not doubted by his clan,
but his skill with the sword is questionable.
Whether he is unable or unwilling to fight
Grendel is unclear; however, his presence in
Heorot, quite alive and rather bitter, suggests that
he does not have so clear a vision
as Beowulf. Yet, it is Unferth who will gift
Beowulf with Hrunting, a mighty blade,
and eventually hail Beowulf as the
savior of the Danes.

Yet Unferth sat at the feast
Covetous of Beowulf's renown.
Mocked him about the rowing match with Breca,
"Seven days and nights you rowed against Breca,

yet he was steady, and he triumphed.
A worse Fate will befall you,
if you challenge Grendel this night!"

AS HERO

I will seek to lead you where others fear to go, teaching you the roads seldom taken from choice. I will be careful of your person and show you the error of your ways. Not all listen whom I advise, but it is better to be wise than brave at times, and this I will show you. When you seek my aid it will be I who guards your back, sees to it that your steps are on the right road, and asks you not only to consider your innermost motives but also to show the understanding you have for those around you. I will not permit you to break faith with yourself or those for whom you care.

AS CHALLENGER

I will always challenge your self-esteem, catching you out in lies and claims that are not true. I will trick you into revealing all that you have hidden, even from yourself. Ask yourself this: Am I who or what I pretend to be? Am I the truest version of myself? Before you undertake the road to the place that has chosen to reveal itself to you, be careful that you do not squander the wisdom you have already found. Be certain that not all who walk the roads of Middle Earth are wise, but know also that many are, and that you are among them.

THE WEAVING OF THE NORNS

HERO

Who fears the old tales of doom and of danger,
Will fall into darkness, his deeds growing dim.
But he who, though weak, or in skill-swerving error,
Takes sword as an heirloom, will reap his reward.
For he who seeks allies to steady his unrede,
Wins the gift of companions in times of great need.

CHALLENGER

Though untruth wraps round you, though taunters traduce you,
Even though bullies bend words to ensnare.
Stand on the ground that your forebears have shown you,
Flinch not, nor fear not; you cannot be moved.
Oak is still oak, and ash a straight javelin,
Lies break their backs against the true spoken word.

8

BRECA

Beowulf's childhood friend,
whom he defeated in a rowing match.
Unferth alludes to the story of their contest,
and Beowulf then relates it in detail.

Seven days and nights
I slipped through the swells,
slaughtering the beasts of the abyss.
Sharp was the swell,
Dreadful were the sea beasts,
but I made the Finnish shore.

AS HERO

It is not easy to swim in the shoals of life. Monsters may lie in wait, and the waters can be rough. Yet, all must do so if they wish to test themselves or come to terms with the issues that surface each day on the journey. You must learn to follow where the waters lead, be guided by their voices, and learn to drink deeply when you need so to do, but to go without water when the time is right. Denying yourself the simpler answers in order to sink deeper into the matter of life will bring you to the place you seek far more swiftly than always striving to find a quick solution. Be aware of your true strengths and weaknesses, for these will tell you much that you need to know.

AS CHALLENGER

However easy the road may seem to you, there will be moments when courage deserts you, when the tests seem too great and the outcome of your journey seems to be of no worth. I will challenge such moments of defeat and show you ways to overcome your deepest doubts. Will you not dance where you seemed before only to stumble? Will you not drive into the deepest waters in order to drink of the wisdom that is there? You may wish to believe only in your own strength, and this may carry you far, but I shall demand yet more of you, for the road is uneven and there are many stones upon it.

THE WEAVING OF THE NORNS

HERO

Hale be the battler, and skilled the contender,
Who holds to the maze of the unwinding game.
Fleet as a dancer, a cunning enchanter,
Carrying the tune of the anthem of fame.
A friend and a fellow to catch and support you;
An ally who'll mirror you fairly and true.

CHALLENGER

Fruitless the struggle to seek and encircle
The one who has woven this wonderful game.
Keep close your craft, lest your hand it betray you,
Feint and consider, seek not to blame.
Fly like the eagle above all contention,
Keen eyed, discover the lie of the land.

KING HRETHEL

When Beowulf is orphaned at the age
of seven, it is King Hrethel who takes the boy
and raises him as a foster son and prince
of the Geats. Hrethel is a loving father and
a generous ring giver. He dies of grief when his
blood son, Herebeald, slays his brother,
Haethcyn, in a hunting accident.

*I was seven winters
when my treasure prince,
lord and friend to his people,
from a lesser father received,
watched over and held me,
Hrethel the One-Eyed King,
gave me riches and a feast,
kinship, and memory.*

AS HERO

Though I have but a single eye, yet I see all things clearly. I have known sorrow, the loss of a child to evil fate, yet I am strong, a gift giver who strives to see where the path leads and will walk before you to make certain your way is clear. Whatever brings you to the great hall of Heorot, I will stand guard for you, strive to bring you to the place of your greatest need, and instruct you in ways to succeed in your endeavors. Always I will look deeply into the past, searching amongst your memories to discover your true goal. Not everything is as it seems.

AS CHALLENGER

Wherever your journey takes you, I shall ask you but one thing: What is your true purpose of coming here? Whatever your answer, I will lead you to the place where you will be most powerfully challenged. Only you know the measure of your resolve. Only you can decide whether to enter whichever one of the realms you are led. At great need I will enter the realm with you, but more often I will send you forth to do battle with your conscience and motivation. Be sure that nothing is as it seems. You may surprise yourself by your answers when challenged in this way. Be aware of the worlds around you, of past and future.

THE WEAVING OF THE NORNS

HERO

Honour the fosterer, he who is father,
Learn well the laws, keeping clan in your heart.
Kin raise the kindred with wealth and affection,
Generous deeds be your helm in the field.
Service sincere shapes each word and each action,
Shelter long-lasting and heartfelt protection.

CHALLENGER

Those who lack love or honest devotion
Look with cold eye on the fear of the heart.
Though you be led to the shores that are barren,
Mercy can flourish, young shoots they can prosper;
Lead well the fosterling, once so discouraged,
Foster love's guidance make a new start.

10

SHIELD SHEAFSON

ᚠ

The legendary Danish king from whom Hrothgar is descended, Shield Sheafson is the mythical founder who inaugurates a long line of Danish rulers and embodies the Danish tribe's highest values of heroism and leadership.

Lo, we Spear-Danes, in days of yore,
we have heard of a great king,
how that strong king won honor and fame!
Of Shield Sheafson, among a scathing host,
many mead seats stole, awing the jarl.
Though first his name was unknown, Fate gifted him
mighty fame under the heavens, honor earned
until each follower over the whale road came,
gave kinship and tribute to a good king

AS HERO

Great hero am I, it is said, from the elder days. Yet, I have known fear, and loss and pain; I have become strengthened though these things. I am, like my name, a shield to my companions, a bulwark against all enemies. I will guide you to places few will venture. I will throw aside the fear and doubts you possess and replace them with new strength and greater determination. At your side I shall bring you to the realm chosen by the Norns, by fate itself. There, I shall offer my wisdom and my wyrd, supporting you in your own journey in search of the truth. Look closely at the tasks that face you. What will they produce? Will you eat the richest food at the table of the gods or seek lesser viands so that your strength takes other forms?

AS CHALLENGER

This challenge I offer you: What do you seek and how will it change your path? Look deeply within yourself to find the hero you may become. Do not deny yourself or your potential but look to the future—remembering that it is also rooted in the past. Deeds that once were may seem poor and forgotten, but others will remember them. Seek the point of balance between hope and despair. Both may teach you. Respect the answers you are given. Challenge yourself.

THE WEAVING OF THE NORNS

HERO

Honour shields you, keeps you brightly,
Stands behind you, holds you strong.
All around you, kinfolk harken
To the old ancestral song.
When day darkens, when night threatens,
Ancient deeds light far your road.

CHALLENGER

When the way is blocked before you,
When your walking comes to halt,
Clutch the stillness, brood the silence,
Listen for the sounding note.
Hear the rallying of horn blast,
Echoing again! Hold fast!'

11

HYGELAC

X

This Geatish king was the son of Hrethel and
brother to Beowulf's mother, making him the hero's
blood uncle and foster brother. Hygelac is a mighty
warrior and battle leader as well; his role as warrior
who is blessed by the gods was perhaps best
exemplified when he arrived just in time to save
a group of Geatish warriors who were being overrun
by the Swedish thanes of King Ongentheow.
The Old English word gealdor, which means
"incantation" or "charm," is used to describe the
horn upon which Hygelac blows when he
arrives to the battlefield.

Refuge came about
that dreadful early dawn
when Hygelac blew his enchanted horn
he knew the Gods would come at last;
That prince had followed a far path.

AS HERO

Listen to the call of my horn! When it is blown it calls great power from the gods. Those who hear it grow stronger. Those I accompany will see much that was hidden. They will be called upon to look within and to see the patterns that shape their lives—from past to present to future, as the Norns decree. I stand at your side and defy the things that make you weak. I give aid to your strength until it is no longer needed. My wisdom grows from the roots of the Great Tree. It carries the weight if the ancestors. Whether you know these or not, they are there. Their wisdom is in your blood, even though you cannot name them. Listen to their song and follow where they lead.

AS CHALLENGER

No matter what you seek, it seldom comes easily or without challenge. This you must accept. Be alert to the circumstances of your quest. What is its true purpose? What is blocking your way? If your need is not worthy, you will fail. What further actions will you take if your path is not open? I will challenge you to find new ways, to seek out new directions that may lead to where you need to be. Not all paths lead to the same place, whatever you may think. Your aim must be true, and your goals chosen with insight and foresight. These are challenges to overcome from the start.

THE WEAVING OF THE NORNS

HERO

*Those who venture where the gods walk
Know their pathways: over, through.
Who would have trustworthy guidance,
Follow in these footsteps true.
Your soul kindred stand beside you,
Incantations to imbue.*

CHALLENGER

*Conflict brings its own confusion,
Craftless lies the helpless victim.
Reft of help, in sad seclusion,
None in saga will depict him:
Bring him into kinship's union
And from sorrow's prison lift him.*

ECGTHEOW

Ecgtheow, Beowulf's blood father, was a member
of the Waegmunding tribe. Ecgtheow's fame
was well known in the northern lands. Ecgtheow's
name indicates a particular skill with a sword,
and he is called a "noble battle leader." During his
younger days, a blood feud arose between Ecgtheow
and the Wulfings tribe after Ecgtheow slew a man from
their kindred. Either the Wulfings refused Ecgtheow's
wergild offer or (more likely) Ecgtheow had nothing of
enough value to offer as wergild to settle the feud.
Ecgtheow found himself an outcast and eventually
found himself in the mead hall of Hrothgar.
A great kinship arose between Hrothgar and Ecgtheow,
and oaths of friendship were sworn by both men.
Hrothgar even paid a proper wergild to the Wulfings
on Ecgtheow's behalf to settle the blood feud.

Of our tribe, Geat people,
and of Hygelac's hearth friends
was my father's kindred known,
noble son of his homeland, Ecgtheow named.
With winters worn, he walked the road to return
to the ancient walls of home; his honor remembered
by wise men within the width of the world

AS HERO

As a father of heroes, I understand well the need to go where you will come face to face with answers to the problems that face you. Having myself suffered the wrath of the fates, who reduced me to the depths of darkness, I have also experienced the strength of friendship, which raised me up once more. Thus will I offer my hand in friendship to you and will guide you on the journey to whatever place fate has prepared for you. Above all I will lead you home, to the place where you are most able to rest and grow strong—no matter what challenges confront you. Honor is the byword in my life; so shall it be in yours.

AS CHALLENGER

All who set foot upon the road to discover the truth of their lives, to divine the meaning of the challenges that confront them, will find me ready to tell them they must dig deeper to find what they are destined to uncover. Though your life may seem broken and your strength at low ebb, I will challenge you to make yet-greater efforts, until you find the kernel of what you seek. Consider what your strengths are, and work with these. Ask yourself what the best way forward will accomplish. And remember that while I challenge you, yet I shall also stand watch by your side.

THE WEAVING OF THE NORNS

HERO

When you stand alone, rejected,
When all your clan account you outlawed,
Seek for friends whose honour shields you,
Helping you to stay supported.
Righting wrongs long unforgiven,
Brings you peacefully back homeward.

CHALLENGER

Scathing words tear down your dwelling,
Envy threadbare name and mantle.
Who seeks your fame, comes fast and felling,
Mountains tumbling to an anthill.
Seek renown by deed and cunning,
Be the byword of men's telling.

HROTHULF

This rather shady character is Hrothgar's orphaned nephew. In Beowulf, after Hrothgar's death, Hrothulf usurps Hrothgar's throne from his sons and declares himself as ruler of the Scyldings. Thus, he is both kin slayer and oath breaker. Heorot will burn because of Hrothulf's betrayal and murder of Hrothgar's sons. The lines below are spoken by Wealtheow, Hrothgar's queen and mother to their young sons, as they celebrate Beowulf's victory in the great hall of Heorot. She sees the shadow upon Hrothulf and worries for the future.

I see my bright shining Hrothulf,
he that had designs for honor to possess,
before when he, prince of the Scyldings,
had a part in the world.
Believe I that he, for the gods and his clan,
will well avenge our children
if he will remember the past,
lo, we did decide and gifted him
before with honor and mercy.

AS HERO

Many will speak ill of me, telling that I usurped the throne of Heorot and brought shame upon the Scyldings. But I will answer that I took what was mine to take, and that as is ever the case, blood was spilled. I am a man who brings to completion what others have failed to do. With me as your guide, I will find the best route to success and bring strength to your endeavours.

Not all paths are what they seem, and not all roads lead to triumph. The weak will often fall by the wayside. But those who journey with full intent will often find themselves raised to ever-greater heights. What you bring to your journey is for you to decide.

AS CHALLENGER

I will seek the best road for you, but it will always be a place where challenges lie in wait to ensnare you, to bring you to a false truth. But I say this also—that you are brought to face these tests for a reason, and that reason is to bring you in time to a place of fulfillment. Your natural strength will bring you honor in times of greatest peril. You shall aspire to great things, and with my help you have a chance to achieve them. Remember also that others may attempt to mislead you. Remember that only within yourself is a true knowledge of your strengths.

THE WEAVING OF THE NORNS

HERO

Whoso seeks to act as leader,
test his purpose, ere you follow.
Look before and test the pathway,
reckoning where it might lead you.
Shadows often, to confuse you,
wear the cloak of a deceiver;
Who will shield you and your kindred,
from the danger that would reive you?

CHALLENGER

Smiles will oft with summer guile you,
seeming honesty enfold you,
Yet the dagger in the darkness
hides a winter in its heart.
False betrayers of the kindred
come as friends to stand usurper.
Sharpen now your keenest cunning;
justice be your firm defender.

14

HRETHRIC
AND HROTHMUND

ᚦ

These are the young sons of Hrothgar and
Wealtheow who will be betrayed by Hrothulf,
their orphaned cousin. The boys are
presented as sitting on either side of Beowulf
while the other youths of Heorot gather around them.
Beowulf, for those moments, is the center of
the young boys' world, a warrior hero who will also
become a father figure to yet another orphan
in the poem, Wiglaf, Weohstan's son.
As Wealtheow gazes upon her sons, fearing
the cold shadow of foreboding in her heart,
Beowulf's presence brings her comfort
and hope for the future.

When turned she to those near,
the bench where her sons were,
Hrethric and Hrothmund, and warrior's sons,
youths together; there sat the good
Beowulf the Geat, by the brothers between.

AS HEROES

Though young, we have seen much of the perils of the world. With us you shall find new ways to learn the truths you need. We shall be as your own sons as we walk with you (even though you have none in Middle Earth), and you may yet find that our innocence is stronger than it appears. As your guides we shall use our natural strengths, or youthful cunning and our joyful love of life to support you on your journey. We shall ask many questions of you as we walk at your side, and our questions will bring forth answers you may not have expected.

AS CHALLENGERS

Our very presence will challenge you. Do we have too few years upon us to know anything of the world? Perhaps so, but we shall ask of you, in return, to consider your own youth, to seek there the answers you have sought as adults. What lies in your childhood that you gave not owned? How will you learn not to repeat the mistakes of your younger days? What relationships led you to this point in your life? Though young and seeming uncertain, yet we are not without wisdom, as are all the young—though this is seldom acknowledged.

THE WEAVING OF THE NORNS

HERO

Youth's the strength that sings abiding,
Faces turned toward the sun,
Life is good while it is growing,
Future days like bean rows sprout.
Doubt is a beetle at heart's vein
Nibbling down what has just begun,
Now's the time to aid, encourage,
Spread protection in and out.

CHALLENGER

Youth's the promising of harvest,
hiding in an ear of wheat;
Stalks that greenly shoot up skyward,
Beaten down by violent storm.
Grain unripened sinks to earth now,
Scattered by one summer's heat.
Patiently to tomb bestowing,
Promising to be reborn.

15

HYGD

Hygelac's queen, Hygd, is a wise and attentive woman. After the defeat of Grendel and Grendel's mother, Hygd graciously greets Beowulf and his warriors upon their victorious return to Geatland. Like Wealtheow, Hygd is both cup bearer and queen, hostess and mother of the clan. Beowulf gifts his queen with three horses and a magnificently jewelled torc (neck ring) from the Danes. Years later, when Hygelac falls in battle, Hygd urges Beowulf to become king of the Geats as she realizes that her son, Heardred, is too immature and unwise to yet be a good leader. Beowulf refuses the throne at that time; instead, he favors young Heardred, and Hygd hesitantly declares her son as chieftain of the Geats. Heardred is killed not long after by the Swedish prince Eanmund, and Beowulf then takes the Geatish throne.

A grand, very valiant queen,
high the hall, Hygd made strong by the journey,
wise, honored, though her winters were few
she remained within the walls,
Hæreþes daughter; not bending,
nor sparing grace from the Geat prince.

AS HERO

I have seen many heroes come and go—some have I welcomed; others turned away. All sought to find favour in my house. Though I seem young to you, those whom I guide will find that I am well versed in the ways of the world, strong willed and generous. I will do my utmost to find solutions, paths that may have been forgotten or overlooked, and guide you to the realm that holds the truth you seek. Much have I learned in my time as a mother. I have looked upon my children and found some to be stronger than others. I have loved them equally but acknowledge that some will go farther than others. So too with you, as we journey together, I offer this truth: we are not all the same—but the goals we set are open to all. Only our true strength will carry us.

AS CHALLENGER

What lies at the centre of your being that troubles you? If you dare to answer this, you will find many doors unlocked. I have seen many who were strong become like water when challenged. Will you face the truths you have hidden from yourself? Will you lend your strength to those in need and show your willingness to share your good fortune? The way is often long and unkind, but the light you carry within brings you to the hearth and home you seek. Will you be glad for this or think it not enough? Only you can answer these things. These are your challenges.

THE WEAVING OF THE NORNS

HERO

Swift is the keeper of heartfelt devotion,
To stand by your side as adviser and sage.
Clear is the vision, as plan is unfolded:
Take up this wisdom for clan and for kin.
Lust to be making each deep undertaking,
Buxom to bend to the bettering gage.
Still to support you, in peace or in conflict,
Hold to this counsel, all precious within.

CHALLENGER

Nagging or subtle, each word like a shuttle,
weaving a cloak on the whale ribs of dream;
Sharp or enchanting, the wheedling message
swirls in the ear like a fly in a horn.
Calmly resolve it, untuning the humming,
lest chaos or conflict unstitch and unseam:
Peaceful and certain, your own counsel taking,
purposely skillful, draw out this sharp thorn.

16

WIGLAF

A young kinsman and retainer
of Beowulf who aids him in the battle against
the dragon while all the other warriors flee in fear.
Wiglaf adheres to the heroic code better than
Beowulf's other retainers, thereby proving himself
a suitable successor to Beowulf.

Wiglaf his name was, Weohstan's son,
Much-loved warrior, the lord of Scyldings,
Aelfhere's kinsman. Saw his lord
Suffering, his masked helmet hot.
He remembered what his lord had gifted,
A rich home with the Waegmundings,
According to every common law, as a father aught.

AS HERO

I carry the light of my heroic lord and bring with it the gifts of strength, honor, and bounty. To all who walk with me, I say to you: I will protect and guide you. I will take you where you need to go and wait while you do what is needful. I will share with you all that I have learned of this life—how to understand the wyrd we are gifted. The spirit of knowing fills me as it fills Beowulf. I offer you the heroes' code: to place the needs of others before your own. Never to flinch in the face of the things that oppose you. To walk forward and not to run from life. To remain open to all things and all paths, and to do all that you can to understand the ways of others.

AS CHALLENGER

To know the ways of others and to honor them can be the hardest part of any path. Yet, this I challenge you to do. Look at the purpose of your journey. Does it carry the needs of others—those who are part of your life? Look for the deeper connections to these. To past as well as present—even to the very doors of the future. Remember that all your actions affect others as well as yourself. Though we may often seem to walk a solitary path, yet we are never truly alone. On this path I walk with you. Others attend on your understanding. Reach out with your thoughts to these—whether distant ancestors or living family and friends. Remember who you are. Remember who they are.

THE WEAVING OF THE NORNS

HERO

Steadfast, undaunted, you keep the bright promises,
No matter the danger, you join in the fray.
To your flag allies will make their glad homages,
Fighting beside you, dark head with the gray.
Leader of levies, no looter of bevies,
Urging on warriors to champion the day

CHALLENGER

Loyalty's leaving is heart faith's deceiving,
False flies the flag on this uncertain field.
Dismiss the dark doubter, lest you be left grieving,
Thankless you'll be if this warrior you wield.
Take to trust's counsel, forbid unbelieving.
State clear your purpose, and this villain will yield.

17

HRUNTING

This is the sword of Unferth, he who first accused
Beowulf of being unworthy of his self-boasting.
After Beowulf slays Grendel, and Grendel's mother
has taken her bloody revenge, Unferth gifts the
sword to Beowulf, seemingly as a gift of friendship
and for success in the battle against Grendel's mother.
Hrunting literally means "thrusting" in Anglo-Saxon,
and on the basis of the poet's description of the blade's
history, it is a mighty weapon. Yet, against Grendel's
mother, Hrunting fails to slay her. That is when Fate
intervenes and another sword, a Giant's sword,
is found by Beowulf and used to finally end the terrorizing
of Heorot by Grendel and his kin.
Although it is an object rather than a character,
the sword has its own personality and may thus
accompany you in your journey.

When mighty help was wanted
then he in need did lend
that hilted sword, Hrunting named.
This was an ancient treasure foremost;
edge of iron, venom to feuds;
never absent from battle, never wandered or untrue
to any man whose life it guarded,
the footsteps of Fate to dare and conquer,
a friend's hall or far battlefield;
it would not be its first journey into the world
another heroic deed destined to do.

AS HERO

To most I am but a weapon in the hands of warriors, yet I have a soul, for I was made with purpose by a great and mighty smith. In your hands I will make you stronger, powerful enough to walk any path to the realm that fate has chosen for you. My presence alone will turn aside negative forces and make clear the way before you. I will also teach you that not all swords are tools of violence but may offer protection for those who carry them, and defense for others. Remember that a sword can bring peace as well as war. My blade is made in magical fire, beaten on the anvil of the fates and tempered to fit the hand of the one who wields me. Your path may also be created for you.

AS CHALLENGER

Remember that once you have set foot upon the path to whichever realm the fates have decreed, there should be no turning back. Though fear may rise before you, you have the strength to face it. Dare to do so. Remember your own courage in setting forth on this road. Own your weaknesses as well as your strengths. There is a hero locked within you. Open your heart to it and become aware of your relationship to the world around you.

THE WEAVING OF THE NORNS

HERO

True is the blade that comes down as gifting,
An heirloom to grasp in the seeker's own hand.
Courage will waken when sword it is shaken,
Vision will rise from the ancestral land.
Wyrd will be sharper, as rhyme of the harper:
Peace weaver you'll be when with cunning you stand.

CHALLENGER

Gift falsely given, reward for no service:
A feint to off-balance, to humble, make sprawl.
Now is the time to awaken, preserve us,
Lest kindred be taken into lies' thrall.
For all that giver appears in good earnest,
There's danger receiving this into your hall.

18

THE STOLEN CUP

A cup stolen from the Dragon's hoard
begins a time of terrible revenge during the last
days of King Beowulf's reign. The dragon is angered
and seeks to destroy those who robbed it.
It is Beowulf's responsibility to end its
reign of terror.

In his grip he held a shining chalice
snatched, not restored—
stolen while the Dragon drowsed
by stealthy ruse:
From the Dragon's storm
king and mortals must speedily amend!

AS HERO

Those who hold me and take me with them also imbibe my wisdom. I was made of ancient gold, drawn from the earth. Though held by the dragon's claw, I was meant for men. I am but one amongst many great treasures, help in thrall but meant to be discovered. As your companion, I offer many things, amongst them honor, truth, and wisdom. These things flow in my depths and are spilled out upon those who hold me and upon the earth where they walk. Follow the gleam of my essence upon your path. Drink deep and be not afraid, for the truth you seek will be born of your efforts, and, as it is said of all heroes, all come home in time.

AS CHALLENGER

When you hold me in your hand, be ready to have your eyes opened. Not all that you may see is treasure. Not all that gleams is gold; not all journeys undertaken are made with vision and good intent. Look to your own reasons and be aware that fate may turn you aside at any moment and place you on another path. Look carefully at the places you are going, and be aware of all that they portend. Ask what truly lies in wait for you. What will you do when the answer you seek is other than the one you hoped for? Will you accept it or deny its truth? Hold me in your hand and let my strength flow through you.

THE WEAVING OF THE NORNS

HERO

"Bold be he who sups with dragons,"
Sings the skald into the night.
Best leave wonders to the hero,
Worn as trophies of his fight.
But if you would breast the waves song,
Start at dawn upon your quest,
Here's the hallow that will bear you
To the company of the blessed.

CHALLENGER

Hold your hand, though treasures beckon:
They are not your own to take.
Anger and revenge will follow
Every movement that you make.
Abide in need and do not hasten—
One stands near you to revoke:
Friend or kindred to forebear you,
Priest or poet to evoke.
Best you leave this plan than hazard
All you own to slip away;
Learn what's yours and what is others,
Lest your faith fall to decay.

19

THE UNFAITHFUL

During Beowulf's last battle with the dragon,
his thanes do the unthinkable: they run and hide,
abandoning their chieftain and comrade,
Wiglaf, in the heat of battle. The warriors do not
emerge from the forest until the dragon
has been slain and their chieftain lies dying
on the ground. These unfaithful thanes
have shattered and broken the warrior
code of the northern clans.

It was not long when
those cowards from the copse came,
oath breakers banded together,
when before none dared the dark magic
despite the gifts of their chieftain and his great need,
but ashamed their shields they bore,
to rush to where on the ground lay,
to gaze on the old king.

AS HEROES

Though we are called heroes by some and cowards by others, yet we offer truths that may not be denied. There are times when to flee is the better part of valor; at others we may say: stand your ground. Only you can know the right course of action; only you know the limits of your courage—though many have found greater reserves than they believed possible. We shall prepare the way for you, for we are as fierce as we are weak. We have walked many roads in our time and know the secret ways between the realms that may one day prove helpful. If you are truly ready for this quest, we shall accompany you, surround you with our swords, and carry all before us—forgetting the dragon and darker days.

AS CHALLENGERS

Are you truly prepared to face your darkest fears, or will you run from them like a coward? Few know of what they are capable, but all the paths have their challenges—as indeed they must; otherwise why would you choose to follow this road? So, too, not all wyrd is good. Sometimes it is better to turn away. But on these paths, you are challenged to keep advancing. In your life, too, you will find moments when you seek to turn back. But to do so brings only greater pain and fear. If you are strong, you will conquer. If not, turn away now.

THE WEAVING OF THE NORNS

HERO

First step's stumble makes men humble,
Causing them to think again;
Wiser no rally without a tally,
When reckoning up the lives of men.
He who holds back spear from flying,
He who knots the wind's own card,
Knows the wiser rede next morning,
Better than the day be marred.
Caution is a wiser counsel,
When no deed can come to good,
Better is a life in hiding,
Than glorious death within the wood.

CHALLENGER

Nithing is the name of nothing,
Nithing is a gap of night
Nithing is the one who promised:
Run away when called to fight.
Nithing speaks, but nothing answers,
Nithing leaves no certain track,
Nithing is the coward's calling,
Nithing turns his faithless back.
Yet, if you can bind the Nithing:
Oaths of fealty, sacred sworn,
Nithing can be something faithful,
And be glad that he was born.

20

THE WAILING WIDOW

Beowulf's funeral is both a sorrowful occasion
and a magnificent celebration of his life.
The Geats mourn their brave ring giver while the
tribe also comes to terms with the betrayal of Beowulf's
war band during the dragon battle. As twelve of
Beowulf's faithful warriors ride around his burial mound
chanting a dirge, a lone female, a widow and
"woman of woe," stands nearby. Her hair is bound for
mourning as she, too, sings a song of lament for
Beowulf. The clear distinction of this figure
as a "widow" could be translated to mean that
she is none other than Beowulf's widow.

Woman of woe,
sang a sorrowful song
mourning the death
of Beowulf of the Geats.
Widowed woman,
with bounden tresses,
sang that dreaded day,

words of slaughter and shame—
she was full of fear.

AS HERO

I have not always known sorrow, though it has come to me now. Thus, I know of the terrors that lie before all, but I am aware also of the joys that were and those that may yet come from even the darkest moments of our lives. If I am chosen to journey with you, I may seem sad and without hope, yet I can bring you past all such terrors and back into the light. If you are lost, journey with me, for I shall find you respite. And if all else fails, I shall sing of your journey, that all may know the way you fought to win your way to your wyrd. I stand close beside you on every step of your way.

AS CHALLENGER

If you stand at the gates of any one of the Nine Realms with sorrow in your heart—how will you proceed? Will you draw upon the strength of those who went before or turn aside and fall back before the seemingly overwhelming forces ranged against you? Many have tried and failed? Will these thoughts whisper in your ear and stop your progress? Or, will you take a moment to consider, knowing that if you do not find the answers you seek now, you may never find them and may never reach a point in your life journey where you can do this. Remember the Norns, remember fate. This is your wyrd.

THE WEAVING OF THE NORNS

HERO

I have listened under moonlight,
I have spoken lover's words,
I have watched the whale roads calling,
I have waved your vessel's sail.
Now I walk under the birch trees,
one of many unmatched birds,
Remembering your arms around me,
like an isle the ocean girds.
Free my hair upon your pillow,
hidden now beneath a veil.
For I am your memory keeper,
one your lonely grave mound guards.

CHALLENGER

Witnessing the fallen hero,
telling forth the tale of pain,
Life that lingers on within me,
raveling out the thread in vain.
But to brightness you would lead me,
gathering up the broken spoil,
Sounds of beauty break upon me
like the shake of golden foil.
Turning to the rain that shimmers
on far horizons long unseen,
I will tear the veil in two now,
uncoil my hair, and be your queen.

THE
WORLD TREE
AND THE NINE
REALMS

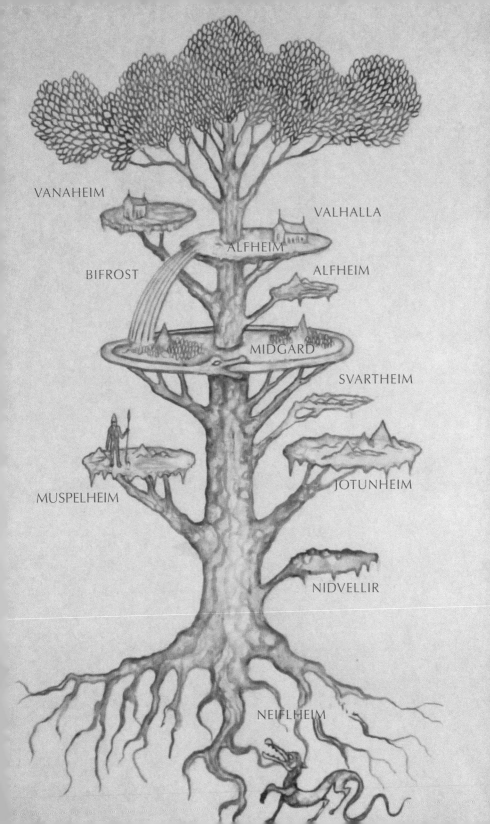

VANAHEIM

VALHALLA

ALFHEIM

BIFROST

ALFHEIM

MIDGARD

SVARTHEIM

MUSPELHEIM

JOTUNHEIM

NIDVELLIR

NEIFLHEIM

THE NINE REALMS

I remember the giants of old
Who gave me bread in those times;
Nine Realms I knew, each in the Tree
With mighty roots under the earth.
—the Elder Edda

Each of these realms has different associations. Each one carries a message that is part of your oracle. The realms, and the qualities they represent, are listed here. The Seeker should note that since your journey begins in Midgard, the ninth destination for *The Beowulf Oracle* is Valhalla, Odin's hall of brave heroes.

ASGARD

TRUTH AND HONOR

From the Old Norse *Ásgarðr*, "enclosure of the Aesir," Asgard is the home of Odin, Frigga, Thor, Loki, and other Aesir. From Asgard, the gods observe all the Nine Realms. Asgard is joined to Midgard by the rainbow bridge, *Bifroest*, where Heimdall stands vigilant as guardian between the worlds.

WYRD SAYING

Those who approach the realm of Asgard do so in search of the gods. They seek to weigh the truth of any matter for which they seek help, and most of all to discover the element of honor that lies within their quest. If you undertake this journey, what are your true motives? Will you honor the answers you are given—the words of the gods and those of the Norns, who hold in their hands the threads of destiny and fate? Will you cross the Rainbow Bridge without fear, or draw upon your courage to step forward, even though your limbs shake and your thoughts are clouded?

NIDVELLIR

TREASURE AND DREAM

From the Old Norse *Nið*, "new moon" or "the wane of the moon," plus *Vellir*, fields." This world is the home of the crafty and magical Dwarves. In the *Voluspa*, the realm is described as having "halls of gold" and being the home of the family of Sindri, a Dwarf whose name is referenced in the *Prose Edda*. This is a dark world, devoid of direct sunlight, and can be interpreted to be a labyrinth of caves leading to many things, including Dwarven treasure.

WYRD SAYING

What treasures do you seek when you come to this realm? Not all treasure is of gold or silver or gems. Wisdom too is a treasure and may be cast in many forms. Listen then—and be aware that all you seek may be hidden from you in the dark but is still before your eyes. Under the new or waning moon, you may find what you are seeking, for these times bring dreams, and in dreams many answers and many treasures are found. Listen and watch with your inner eyes and you shall learn more than all the striving for wealth of whatever kind that has guided your steps hitherto.

NEIFLHEIM

LOSS AND TRANSFORMATION

From the Old Norse *Niflheimer*—"world of fog." An icy land of mist and shadow that is also known as the home of Hel, one of Loki's daughters. Those who do not die a heroic death in battle come here to spend their afterlife. This is not a punishment but rather an alternative path for those who do not die with a sword in their hand. Along with the departed, the Seeker may also encounter a poisonous spring called Hvergelmir, from which flowed many rivers. These frozen rivers are known as Élivágar. Eventually the poisonous substance within the flow came to harden and turn to ice, which is the fifth sacred element of the northern lands and perhaps represents the metaphysical transformation that can occur in this realm.

WYRD SAYING

Much may be hidden before it is revealed. In this realm, many choices are set before you. This is a place of purification, where old patterns and stories are purged to make way for new. Those who come here seek restoration and vitality. They are offered it when they are willing to see that old patterns must be let go of, and that new friendships may be made. The strength of kinship is important to all who seek progress. Old ways are not always best. Children must grow and become men or women. Old links must be undone.

VANAHEIM

HIDDEN MEMORY AND MAGIC

In Old Norse, *Vanahemir*—"homeland of the Vanir." In Vanaheim, the Vanir—gods even older than the Aesir—dwell in a world full of magic. Vanaheim is somewhat hidden in that a direct path is unknown to exist. Here the Seeker will find the wisdom of the Vanir and many paths of mystery and magic.

WYRD SAYING

The gods before the gods dwell in this realm. Their wisdom is ancient and ancestral. But the path is a hard one, and the secrets of this realm are well hidden. You may need to try harder to find an answer, but be sure that when or if you do, it will be of great value. Be aware of your true motives at all times when journeying to this realm, for falsehood and evil thoughts are quickly discovered and answers will not come. Seek with an open heart and clearness of mind and the Vanir will answer.

MUSPELHEIM

VISION AND CREATION

From the Old Norse, *Múspellsheimr*—"the world of Muspell." A bright and flaming place, this realm is the home of the Fire Giants. The many flames of this realm are fueled with the powers of creation and transformation, beginning and end, life and death. These are the fires that burn so hot that only the chosen may enter. This is the realm where visions come to be and are then gifted to the shaman and *völva*.

WYRD SAYING

Here you may seek not only truth, but true vision, which is not the same. Vision opens the doors of inner sight and brings true seeing that is not always given to mortals. Here, where the fires of inspiration are easily kindled, those energies that enable the creation of great things and even greater wonders are yours to access. When you are in this realm, you will see and hear with clarity, and the words you utter will be filled with power that others will recognize.

JOTUNHEIM

WISDOM & STRENGTH

From the Old Norse, *Jötunheimr*—"World of the Giants." This is a wild place where chaos thrives; indeed, this is a landscape of dark, thick forests and tall, craggy mountains. Here the Giants thrive with their fierce strength and brute force. These are ancient beings who have witnessed many cycles of creation and destruction. A great stronghold called Utgaard protects the realm, and a river named Ifing separated it from the realm of Asgard. Here also was Mimir's well—the source of the gods' wisdom. Here, in their realm, the Seeker will find many paths that have no shortage of challenges.

WYRD SAYING

Those who come to this realm come in arch of strength—even if they do not know their need. Strength that will carry them through times of hardship or despair, strength to recover from hurt and harm. But they know also that there is wisdom to be found here—for herein lies Mimir's well, the source of the wisdom that feeds the world tree and brings empowerment to all who drink from it. Even the gods draw wisdom from this sacred well. Here, too, come those in search of protection, for within the walls of the mighty fortress of Utgaard, no darkness or shadow or cold breath of iron may come.

ALFHEIM

LUCK AND DESTINY

From the Old Norse, *Álfheimr*—"homeland of the Elves," Alfheim is home to the Lios Alfar or Light Elves. They are fairer to look upon than the sun and bring great luck to those who encounter them. Their beauty is almost beyond our imagining as mere mortals. One may see this as a realm filled with music, where song and poetry are composed with full heart. Alfheim is the land of Freyr, a Vanir god, although the mystery of how this came to be and how the Elves and Freyr coexist can be solved only by the Seeker who walks these paths.

WYRD SAYING

Luck and destiny are not the same, though they're often thought to be so. Luck is random, but destiny is shaped by the gods—though even so, we are not bound upon the wheel that turns forever. On the great tree of Yggdrasil, men climb and fall, reaching places to which they were destined to come, and grow to understand that their true place in the pattern is not always what they seek. Even so, many will reject the truth and seek other paths. Here you may find dance and song, poetry, and skills to shape metals and stone. Your dreams may expand beyond imagining, and your hopes ring out loudly in Middle Earth.

SVARTHEIM

POWER AND CUNNING

In Norse mythology, *Svartálf[a]heimr,* "home of the dark elves," is the place of the Svart Alfar. As their name suggests, these are the shadow kind amongst the Elves. Possessed of great strength and vision, they have little love for humankind and will often stir up bad feelings and negative energies for those who visit them. They are, however, wise and cunning and may offer seemingly harsh advice that yet lends itself to great returns.

WYRD SAYING

Many avoid this realm, knowing it as a place of trickery and deceit. But though it is true that the dark elves are not always truthful and do not always like humankind, they are possessed of great wisdom from a deeply ancient time. So, come and learn, but beware of being misled or having your dreams of aggrandizement spurred on until they bring ruin upon you. If your inner strength enables you to pass by these things, then the path will open before you in ways you may not expect or even understand. Walk with caution and keep your thoughts from dark places.

VALHALLA

REST AND ACHIEVEMENT

For Beowulf and the warriors of the North, spending the afterlife in the great hall of Odin, the hall of the brave, was the ultimate life reward. All heroes deemed worthy of the honour are taken here after their death to spend eternity feasting on the finest foods, drinking the best mead, and fighting the mightiest enemies. Here, in this realm of *The Beowulf Oracle*, the Seeker will find a mighty mead hall, sturdy and vast, filled with the greatest warrior heroes from the North: Beowulf, Sigurd, Gudrun, and more.

WYRD SAYING

The place of rest and triumph after struggle. Those who come to Valhalla have been on a journey of great courage and fortitude. Not all reach here, and many who do are turned away or find that what they sought was but an empty shell. Those who are brought forward, who find acknowledgment for the wisdom they carry within, will be welcomed into the mead hall and awarded with the greatest prizes of all: honour and truth.

five

WORKING WITH
THE BEOWULF ORACLE

Having spent time getting to know the cards and the characters in the oracle, you are now ready to work with it. Below you will find some additional ideas to add to your experience and to deepen the answers you receive.

Greeting & Thanking the Norns

The following brief ceremony is to help you create a deeper link between yourself and the Norns.

Place the three Norn cards in a row on a suitable surface (you may be able to find or make a stand that will enable them to be upright). Place a tea light or candle in front of them. If possible, add a sprig of greenery, especially from an ash tree if one grows nearby and you can find fallen twigs without taking a cutting.

Once you have created your shrine, stand or sit before it and say these words (or others of your own devising):

> Great Wisdom Keepers,
> Norns,
> Holders of wyrd—
> I greet you.

I offer my thanks
For your presence.
I offer my thanks
For your wisdom.
I offer my thanks
For your guidance.
I offer my thanks
For your truth.

I ask that
You guide my steps
Into deeper awareness.
I ask that you give
The gift of true seeing.

If you wish, you now may enter into meditation, seeking further contact with the Norns, or simply sit with them in silence for a time. When you are ready, thank the Norns, blow out the candle, and replace the cards in the pack.

THE HEOROT SPREAD

This spread is designed to help you choose a Hero or Challenger.

Heorot is the focus for the action in much of the original poem. It resounds to stories of heroic exploits and later to the cries of fear and terror as the monsters Grendel and Grendel's mother stalk and destroy the men and women in the hall.

Such halls followed a standard pattern throughout the period from the sixth to the ninth centuries. Long and narrow, the hall was divided into two rows of benches, facing across a table (or sometimes a fire trench) and with the leader seated at the head of the table. Servants then brought food and drink along the sides of the hall, filling trenchers and cups.

In this spread we imagine ourselves entering such a hall. Shuffle and lay out twelve cards, facedown in two rows of six, facing each other as if they were seated at the table. Place the three Norn cards, again facedown, as follows: one at the head of the table, one in the centre, and the third at the foot of the table.

When you have decided on your question—or if you are preparing for a journey—turn over a card from one of the two rows. This represents you. Then select the card facing you across the table and turn that over, to represent your Hero or Challenger. (Alternately, you can select either one of the cards sitting next to you at the table.) Consider which you want this Companion to be—do you feel the need to be supported or challenged? Much depends on the nature of your question. If you are feeling weak, you might welcome a champion to support you; if you are in a strong place but still feel conflicted, a challenger may help you recover your balance.

Read these two cards (or more if you choose a Hero *and* a Challenger) first, then, following your intuition, turn over one of the three Norn cards and read the Weaving of the Norns for your companion. You may find yourself directed toward one of the Nine Realms, in which case look up the meaning in the book. This will help you make any additional conclusions, and need not always be followed unless clearly required by the Norn.

There are several alternate ways you can work with this layout, choosing more Hero or Challenger cards to support or question you on your journey.

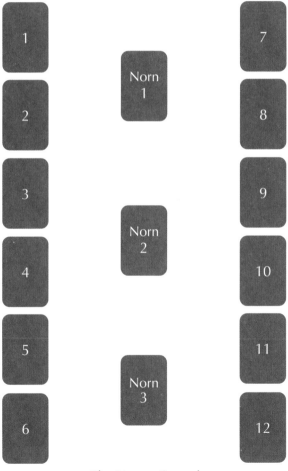

The Heorot Spread

Here is a sample reading using this spread.

The client was an inventor who had been made a proposal to collaborate on developing an already-existing product that he had designed and crafted. He sought advice about the value or otherwise of this offer.

Having laid out the cards as shown on p. 139, he drew card **5** from the left-hand row of cards. This was **Breca.** He then selected the card facing him—number **11**—**Shield Sheafson.** He decided that Breca should challenge him and Shield Sheafson should be his champion.

He then read the message from Breca as Challenger:

Wherever your journey takes you, I shall ask you but one thing: What is your true purpose of coming here? Whatever your answer, I will lead you to the place where you will be most powerfully challenged. Only you know the measure of your resolve. Only you can decide whether to enter whichever one of the realms you are led. At great need I will enter the realm with you, but more often I will send you forth to do battle with your conscience and motivation. Be sure that nothing is as it seems. You may surprise yourself by your answers when challenged in this way. Be aware of the worlds around you, of past and future.

He felt that in the current moment, the way forward was too much for his courage, but the questions posed by Breca were helpful in that they suggested how he might come through, despite the way being filled with uncertain problems.

Now he turned to Shield Sheafson as Hero. He read:

Great hero am I, it is said, from the elder days. Yet, I have known fear, and loss and pain, I have become strengthened though these things. I am, like my name, a shield to my companions, a bulwark against all enemies. I will guide you to places few will venture. I will throw aside the fear and doubts you possess, and replace them with new strength and greater determination. At your side I shall bring you to the realm chosen by the Norns, by fate itself. There, I shall offer my wisdom and my wyrd, supporting you in your own journey in search of the truth. Look closely at the tasks that face you. What will they produce? Will you eat the richest food at the table of the gods or seek lesser viands so that your strength takes other forms?

From this, he felt offered good advice and the best way to overcome his doubts. Especially useful was the question about what would be produced by the tasks before him.

Now he turned to the Norns for confirmation and turned over **Skuld**, who represents "What Shall Be." Reading the weavings for each card he got, for Breca as Challenger:

> *Fruitless the struggle to seek and encircle*
> *The one who has woven this wonderful game.*
> *Keep close your craft, lest your hand it betray you,*
> *Feint and consider, seek not to blame.*
> *Fly like the eagle above all contention,*
> *Keen eyed, discover the lie of the land.*

While for Shield Sheafson as Hero, he saw this:

> *Honour shields you, keeps you brightly,*
> *Stands behind you, holds you strong.*
> *All around you, kinfolk harken*
> *To the old ancestral song.*
> *When day darkens, when night threatens,*
> *Ancient deeds light far your road.*

In the first he latched upon the counsel to "keep close your craft," and to "feint and consider" and be "keen eyed." The Norn's words for Shield Sheafson as Hero bid him maintain the honor of his ancestors and what they had produced in the past. From this, he felt he would cautiously consider the proposal but keep his options open, maintaining good boundaries around how the collaboration might work. In the end this proved of great value, and the prototype of his invention is currently on a secure production line.

THE NORN SPREAD

For a quick answer when such is required, use this:

Simply draw one Norn and one Companion card from the deck. Place them side by side and read the text from the book. Though the presence of the Norn is to bear witness to the divination, depending on which card is drawn the matter in question may fall into What Once Was, What Is Coming into Being, and What Shall Be. As always, consider your own responses to the imagery. Look into the eyes of the archetype and listen for its voice.

Here is a sample reading using this spread:

The client was a woman seeking advice concerning a partner in her life who was being very cool and distant toward her. She asked why he was behaving like this, and what, if anything, she could do to solve the issue.

She drew a Companion card randomly after shuffling the pack. It was **Hygelac.** She decided to work with him as a Challenger, seeking fresh ways to reach a place of healing and restoration for her and her partner.

The Challenger's message was clear:

No matter what you seek, it seldom comes easily or without challenge. This you must accept. Be alert to the circumstances of your quest. What is its true purpose? What is blocking your way? If your need is not worthy, you will fail. What further actions will you take if your path is not open? I will challenge you to find new ways, to seek out new directions that may lead to where you need to be. Not all paths lead to the same place, whatever you may think. Your aim must be true, and your goals chosen with insight and foresight. These are challenges to overcome from the start.

This led her to consider the basis of her relationship—what was its true purpose? What was blocking it? Her challenge was to find new ways, new paths that might yield unexpected surprises. Keeping time to this purpose was the clue!

The Weaving of the Norn for Hygelac as Challenger spoke of her partner feeling sad and excluded:

Conflict brings its own confusion,
Craftless lies the helpless victim.
Reft of help, in sad seclusion,
None in saga will depict him:
Bring him into kinship's union
And from sorrow's prison lift him.

She did not have to ponder long on the advice of the Norn, since it concerned a debate they had when they first came together—that they would not marry but simply live together. The woman had been previously in a bad marriage and, at the time her new partner and she met, had been reluctant to marry again. Now, two years in, she was feeling more secure. The Norn she had chosen, **Skuld,** stood for "What Shall Be," which pointed to a new future. Following the divination, the couple talked about the possibility of a simple civil partnership—a decision that changed everything for them both.

THE HRUNTING SPREAD

This spread is designed to help you see your journey more clearly and the elements of that journey more clearly. Hrunting literally means "thrusting" in Anglo-Saxon, and the description of the sword's history reveals that it is a formidable weapon. These blades were more than weapons; they were often family heirlooms, handed down from hero to hero. They were mighty gifts from chieftain to warrior. Songs and poems were often devoted to the tale of a sword and its deeds.

In this spread, imagine a sword being handed to you for this journey. Shuffle and lay out ten cards, facedown, as in the diagram on the next page. Turn over the top card. This represents the Courage Call. This is what you yearn for, learn of, or experience as a challenge. Reveal the second card, Kinship, which is what or who will accompany you for this journey. Cards 3, 4, and 5 represent what you will encounter during the first part of your own heroic journey: card 3 is the Sea Steed, or what or who you need to cross the whale road successfully, which is the next card. Card 4, the Whale Road, is what you must cross in order to progress toward the Courage Call from card 1. Card 5 is the Raven's Eye, which reveals what or whom you will meet, possibly a reunion, on the whale road.

Cards 6, 7, and 8 represent the steps of the journey. Card 6 is the Heart of the Blade card and represents the crux of the matter at hand. Card 7 is the Afflicter of Men and reveals what is directing a threat/change/danger to the Heart of the Blade. Card 8 is Memory's Way, where the Seeker is reminded of, learns of, or shares something from the past that helps to establish the Seeker's place in the journey.

Finally, cards 9 and 10 symbolize the challenge and the outcome of the journey. Card 9 is the Shadow Breaker and reveals the Seeker's challenge in its rawest, purest form. Card 10 is the Farthest Shore and shows the outcome.

The Hrunting Spread

Here is a sample reading using this spread.

The client was unsure whether taking an actual, physical journey in the near future would be possible and, perhaps more importantly, if it was necessary and prudent.

Having laid out the cards as shown in the diagram, card 1 was **Wiglaf**. This card revealed the **Courage Call** to connect with loyalty from or to allies and friends or the home of friend or family. Card 2, **Kinship**, was **Hrethel**, who symbolizes protection, a "home away from home" or perhaps an adopted family. Clearly, the physical journey is for and because of a family/friend, and there will be a close friend or family member who will accompany the client on this journey.

The Dragon was card 3, the **Sea Steed**. This card reveals that the path or method of making the journey will be tenacious, intimidating, and possibly even dangerous. Card 4, the **Whale Road,** the actual path of the journey, is **Hygelac**. This card shows that the Seeker's journey is blessed by the gods and they will receive a *gealdor* (charm or incantation), which may be a physical item or a chant, song, or poem, to guide and ensure safe passage.

The steps of the journey as revealed in cards 6, 7, and 8 were as follows: the **Heart of the Blade**, the foundation of the journey, was the **Hrothulf** card. The Seeker will meet or has met a shadowy influence that warns them to place kinship above ambition. Card 7, the **Afflicter of Men**, was the **Hrothgar** card. This revealed that within this portion of the journey there exists a challenge from without that will (and perhaps necessarily) destroy that which is. Card 8, **Memory's Way**, showed the card of **Unferth**, revealing that the challenge or challenger from card 7 exists very close to the Seeker.

The athanor of the challenge, the **Shadow Breaker**, was revealed in card 9 as the **Unfaithful**. The challenge or challenger is a group or member of a known group that will not stand fast (or did not stand fast) with the Seeker when they are, or were, most needed. Finally, the **Farthest Shore**, the outcome, was the **Beowulf** card, symbolizing that the Seeker will be successful and well rewarded.

As a result of the reading, the client postponed the trip until a storm system had cleared, and she chose to take a trusted family member with her on the trip. Rather than fly and reduce the time of travel, she elected to drive a rental car since her own vehicle was older and prone to its own quirks. Rather than stopping at an "old friend's" house along the way, which had been discussed, she decided to skip that visit and a possible awkward situation.

In the end, the client's journey was safely completed, and she arrived at her destination without incident. When she arrived, she was pleasantly surprised with a special dinner and plans to attend a museum exhibit that especially interested her.

THE RUNE MESSAGES

Each of the Companion cards has a rune from the Norse runic Futhark alphabet. When used in conjunction with the regular meanings of the cards, they can add to the reading of the wyrd. You can also use the following method as an alternative way to consult the oracle.

Hold all of the Companion cards facedown in one hand. Concentrate on your question and let that energy flow into the cards as you shuffle them. Place the cards on a flat surface, spread them out, and ask your question again. Choose three cards and turn them over. Read the oracle's message for each card. Below, you will find a rune message for each card, as well as a brief description of the rune. We have listed these by Companion card for quick reference.

Beowulf—Tiwaz

RUNE MEANING: Justice and sacrifice; this is the rune of the Norse warrior god, Tyr. The rune symbolizes the rule of law and peacekeeping.

HERO: *Know well the sword and the hand that wields it. I walk with the hero as weapon and inspiration. I call for sacrifice, and it must be paid. Do not be overcome with loss. Oftentimes sacrifice will invoke a new dawn.*

CHALLENGER: *Courage cannot be found. The price is too high. Overwhelmed and ill equipped. The cause of conflict may be unjust or veiled in a fog of misunderstanding. Wait for the truth before drawing your sword.*

Hrothgar—Ansuz

RUNE MEANING: Order and breath; this is a rune of the Norse Allfather, Odin. The rune symbolizes our elders and inspiration.

HERO: *Sage and wise one of Odin. I am wisdom and hindsight. Through battle and strife, I have earned my reputation as a wise and cunning leader. I have many gifts for those who are worthy. Listen well to my words. Observe me with a keen eye.*

CHALLENGER: *Foolish one of false reputation. Beware their oaths and promises of fame and fortune. This is not the one. Continue your search for wisdom.*

Grendel—Hagalaz

RUNE MEANING: Catalyst for change and disruption; this is a rune of chaos and confrontation. The rune symbolizes crisis and opportunity.

HERO: *The unmoving shall be moved. The time has come to confront and move obstacles before you. Gain control. The past, no matter how terrible, is beyond your grasp. Release the resentment. Take that first brave step.*

CHALLENGER: *Your test is one of stillness and patience. Look all around you. Consider every piece of the situation. Weigh your choices. What must change before you can truly move forward?*

Grendel's Mother—Othala

RUNE MEANING: Inheritance and legacy; this is a rune of clan hierarchy and the balance of a happy home. The rune symbolizes ancestral power and inheritance.

HERO: *The wronged will be avenged; gather your kin and draw strength from one another. Retrieve what was taken; it belongs with your tribe. Make offerings to the ancestors. They will guide you.*

CHALLENGER: *When blood kin prove false, open the doors for them to depart. If deemed unworthy, do not allow your kin to taint your path with their chosen poison. Love from a distance. The needs of the clan must be first in your decision.*

The Dragon—Kenaz

RUNE MEANING: Fire and transformation; this is a rune of illumination and growth. The rune symbolizes transformation and exploration.

HERO: *Step into the crucible. Do not fear the heat; transformation is coming. Enlightenment will follow. Embrace the flame.*

CHALLENGER: *There is nothing for you behind the wall of flame; do not fight the fire simply because you know how to quench it. Do not engage.*

Wealtheow—Uruz

RUNE MEANING: Persistence and survival; this is a rune of determination and will. The rune symbolizes life force and endurance.

HERO: *Own the power that is yours; embrace it and learn to wield it gently yet firmly. Be subtle yet swift when you act.*

CHALLENGER: *Although you can see the many paths of possibility, the outcome is beyond your control. Do not lament this or count this as a woe; your awareness and keen sight will allow you to prepare for what is to come.*

Unferth—Thurisaz

ᚦ

RUNE MEANING: Weapon and defense; this is a rune of the Norse god Thor. The rune symbolizes unconscious forces and the forces of society.

HERO: *Sharp and cunning, quick with wit. Ever watchful, an ally I am. I read the battle runes as I sit at the king's feet.*

CHALLENGER: *My taunts are to test your mettle; a thorn to your side. I shine a light into the darkness, the hidden places, and reveal any lie to match the boast and brag.*

Wiglaf—Ehwaz

ᛖ

RUNE MEANING: Initiation and immortality; this is a rune of steadfastness and mystery. The rune symbolizes endurance and enlightenment.

HERO: *Be unwavering in your oaths; let no one and no thing call you away from the path that is before you now. Stand fast. Courage!*

CHALLENGER: *Words spoken in haste; promises made but cannot be kept. My absence in your time of need will be profound.*

Breca—Mannaz

RUNE MEANING: Memory and learning; this is a rune of strategy and structure. The rune symbolizes humankind and potential.

HERO: *I am your match in strength and prowess. Forever friend, battle brother, oar dancer. I bring forth the best in you and everyone around me.*

CHALLENGER: *My battle frenzy will drive you forward into the fray with little thought for the outcome. Beware my thirst for confrontation. Soothe my passion before stepping into my circle.*

Hrethel—Algiz

RUNE MEANING: Protection and teaching; this is a rune of safety and listening. The rune symbolizes divinity and spiritual connection.

HERO: *I am your guide and protector. My home has a safe hearth for you. I am your honored ancestor; my lessons are of fairness and honor. Teacher, guardian, parent. I will walk with you or carry you, whichever I must.*

CHALLENGER: *I have little of value to teach you, though I will promise otherwise. My lessons are unnecessarily harsh. What I can show you can be learned from another with a cost that is not so high.*

Shield Sheafson—Fehu

RUNE MEANING: Wealth and beginnings; this is a rune of personal power and prosperity. The rune symbolizes abundance and reputations.

HERO: *I am the first, the one who paved the path for my people to prosper. Battle winner. Father figure. Family founder. I am the deep root of tradition.*

CHALLENGER: *My foundation is weak. The timbers of my hall are rotting and creak ominously. Strengthening me will require a high price from you.*

Hygelac—Gebo

RUNE MEANING: Exchange and generosity; this is a rune of gratitude and gifting. The rune symbolizes hospitality and balance.

HERO: *The door to my hall is open to you; here you will find welcome and the warmth of kinship. Knowledge. Growth. They are my gifts to you.*

CHALLENGER: *My gifts are tarnished; my sword is dull. You will find my* *hall to be cold and fireless. Do not linger here; you will only become chilled and motionless.*

Ecgtheow—Nauthiz

RUNE MEANING: Need and necessity; this is a rune of life lessons and consequence. The rune symbolizes hard work and self-reliance.

HERO: *Stand firm in your convictions and listen to the voices of the ancestors. Push hard. Raise your shield. Let the first stroke be theirs; let the last stroke be yours.*

CHALLENGER: *Want is quenched well before need; the repetition of ill choices results in a backward path. Look inward and awaken the ancestors.*

Hygd—Jera

RUNE MEANING: Harvest and patience; this is a rune of peace and plenty. The rune symbolizes cycles and effort.

HERO: *Wait. Listen. Focus. See the possibilities before you and consider them all. Careful. Patient. Silent. There is little value in haste for you here.*

CHALLENGER: *I advise swift action and sharpened swords. Change is inevitable; do not delay what is to come, for it is coming. Do not be late to the battle.*

Hrothulf—Isa

RUNE MEANING: Stillness and self-control; this is a rune of focus and self-image. The rune symbolizes identity and stasis.

HERO: *I sit in shadows and silence while abiding my station. I know well my place in the king's hall, as do all who dwell within. My voice is seldom heard. Look to my icy stare to know what it is that I desire.*

CHALLENGER: *I have a face that is easily forgotten; I am a name that cannot be remembered. A song not sung; a story seldom told.*

Hrethric and Hrothmund—Wunjo

RUNE MEANING: Hope and joy; this is a rune of fellowship and friendship. The rune symbolizes expectation and community.

HERO: *I am the future; I am where your hope lies for peace and balance. Nurture me. Guide me. Share your knowledge and experience with me. I look to you for protection. Together, we will find fellowship.*

CHALLENGER: *I cannot be the fulfillment of your dreams; do not burden me with a task that is yours. I am not you and will never be. Accept me as I am or forever find me less.*

Hrunting—Sowilo

RUNE MEANING: Victory and wholeness; this is a rune of confidence and action. The rune symbolizes success and motivation.

HERO: *My lineage is one of victory in battle; my bite is keen and deep. With my venom I will bring your enemies to their knees. Wield me with joy of battle; hear my battle song as together we destroy that which stands in our way.*

CHALLENGER: *I cannot be your only weapon; I will serve you until I cannot. My end will bring another; hold fast to it and wield it well.*

The Stolen Cup—Inguz

RUNE MEANING: Seed and process; this is a rune of evolution and space. The rune symbolizes creation and development.

HERO: *I am the beginning, the first step, the first choice. My keeper is not my master. I am one of many, but most see only the one. Admire from afar; return if found lost.*

CHALLENGER: *All stops here. There is no path forward except one in which you are blind and deaf. Find another way.*

The Unfaithful—Perthro

RUNE MEANING: Fate and fortune; this is a rune of chance and interaction. The rune symbolizes the unknowable.

HERO: *Alone you must stand when the battle breaks. I am near. Just out of sight. Just out of reach. I am here. I am close. I will come.*

CHALLENGER: *I stand at the edge and call down to you; a great river divides us; a mountain stands between us. Keep moving. I will be here at the end.*

Wailing Widow—Berkano

RUNE MEANING: Rebirth and healing; this is a rune of mature wisdom and fertility. The rune symbolizes safety and sanctuary.

HERO: *Weep as needed; let your heart mourn. Feel no shame in your keening; all nine worlds share in your loss. Know that death is only the beginning.*

CHALLENGER: *Your sadness is too long lived; release the grief. Let go the anger. Your weeping has filled the rivers over much. You may rest now and heal. Draw comfort from the Allmother.*

With this we wish you well in your explorations in the world of *The Beowulf Oracle*. May your journeys to the Nine Realms and your meetings with the Norns be fruitful and full of wisdom, and may fate smile upon you and gather you into the circle of the Great Tree.

FURTHER READING AND RESOURCES

The Original Poem

If you would like to look at the original manuscript, go to the British Library online website and you will find a digitized copy. www.bl.uk (search collection-items > beowulf)

Hobson, Jacob. "An Old Norse Courtly Analogue to *Beowulf.*" *Neophilologus* 103, no. 4 (2019): 577–590. https://doi.org/10.1007/s11061-019-09601-0

Lesslie Hall, P. D. *The Project Gutenberg E-book of Beowulf.* Retrieved from Project Gutenberg: http://www.gutenberg.org (2005).

And for those who would like to hear what the poem sounded like, the following DVD recording is fascinating.

Bagby, Benjamin (voice and Anglo-Saxon harp). *Beowulf.* Koch Vision, 2006. 2006KOC-DV-6445.

Translations of the Poem

There are many fine translations of *Beowulf.* These are the ones we found most useful while working on the oracle.

Crossley-Holland, Kevin, trans. *Beowulf.* Oxford: Oxford University Press, 1999.

Heaney, Seamus, trans. *Beowulf: A New Translation.* London: Faber & Faber, 1999.

Tolkien, J. R. R., trans. *Beowulf: A Translation and Commentary, Together with Sellic Spell.* Edited by Christopher Tolkien. New York: HarperCollins, 2014.

BOOKS ON NORSE MYTHOLOGY
AND BACKGROUND STUDIES OF BEOWULF

Clark-Hall, J. R. *A Concise Anglo-Saxon Dictionary for the Use of Students*. London: Andesite, 2015.

Gaiman, Neil. *Norse Mythology*. London: Bloomsbury, 2018.

Grigsby, John. *Beowulf & Grendel*. London: Watkins, 2005.

Hobson, Jacob. "An Old Norse Courtly Analogue to *Beowulf*." *Neophilologus* 103, no. 4 (2019): 577–90.

Hughes, Amy. *Norse Mythology: Learn about Viking History, Myths, Norse Gods, and Legends*. Bari, Italy: Fabrizio Bellomo, 2020.

Mountfort, Paul Rhys. *Nordic Runes: Understanding, Casting, and Interpreting the Ancient Viking Oracle*. Rochester, VT: Destiny Books, 2003.

Seigfried, Karl E. H. "Beowulf: History, Legend, and Mythology." Digital Collections for the Classroom. https://dcc.newberry.org/collections/beowulf_history_legend_and_mythology.

Sturluson, Snorri. *The Prose Edda: Norse Mythology*. Edited and translated by Jesse L. Byock. New York: Penguin Classics, 2006.

Sutcliffe, Rosemary. *Beowulf: Dragonslayer*. London: Puffin Books, 2016.

Thomsen, Brian M. *The Further Adventures of Beowulf: Champion of Middle Earth*. New York: Carroll & Graf, 2006.

Tolkien, J. R. R. *The Monsters and the Critics and Other Essays*. London: HarperCollins, 2007.

ABOUT THE AUTHORS AND ARTIST

John Matthews is an independent writer, researcher, and *New York Times* bestselling author who has devoted much of the past 40 years to the study of Arthurian traditions, the Grail, and myth in general. He has produced a number of successful divinatory systems based on early spiritual beliefs, including *The Arthurian Tarot, The Wildwood Tarot, The Grail Tarot,* and *The Tarot of Light and Shadow*. He has won several awards, some of his titles have been recommended by the New York Public Library, and he is a regular guest at Tarot conferences. Visit www.hallowquest.org.uk.

Virginia Chandler is an American author who lives in the Deep South of Georgia. She cowrote *The Last Dragon of the North* and recently released *The Green Knight's Apprentice,* both with Double Dragon Publishing. She recently collaborated with John and Caitlin Matthews on the bestselling *Arthurian Magic* (Llewellyn, 2017) and has completed the book *Year of the Magickal Dragon* (Llewellyn, 2020). She has spent many years studying Anglo-Saxon literature and mythology, knowledge of which she brings to this project.

Joe Machine is a world-renowned artist and founding member of the Stuckist movement. Joe's work has been widely exhibited and received praise from art critics such as Edward Luci-Smith. Much of his work focuses on myth and legend. His recent illustrations for *Britannic Myths* by Steven O'Brien received critical acclaim. He is currently preparing an exhibition on themes from the Arthurian legends. He lives in Somerset with his wife and children.